April
East

**A bawdy, biting and witty satire
of show business and celebrity.**

A NOVELLA BY
JOE STOCKDALE

HB

Hyphenates Books

Published by Hyphenates Books[sm]
A division of Hyphenates, Ltd.
P.O Box 3771
Danbury Connecticut 06813

First Printing, May 2014
10 9 8 7 6 5 4 3 2 1

Copyright © 2014 Joe Stockdale
ISBN: 0983882576
ISBN: 9780983882572
LIBRARY OF CONGRESS CATALOGING-IN-PUBLICATION DATA: 2014934514
Hyphenates, Limited, Danbury, CT

Hyphenates Books is a service mark of Hyphenates, Ltd.

Front cover art: Nathan Striedinger

Printed in the United States of America

PUBLISHER'S NOTE
This is a work of fiction. Names, characters, places, and incidents either are the
product of the author's imagination or are used fictitiously, and any resemblance to
actual persons, living or dead, business establishments, events, or locales is entirely
coincidental.

DEDICATION

In honor of "the pillow plumpers" who, as with most back stage workers, get no respect, but provide the set dressing and hand props for every production.

"He gulped and looked again at the movie poster. April Barlow had gorgeous breasts. In her picture she always wore gowns cut down low at the neck. You could often see the little groove between the two delectable promontories of her bust. Her hips were ample, too. They swayed when she walked even better than those of April East who was corseted a little too tightly, and she had a way of looking at a man with her lips parted and her eyes opened wide..."

From: "Ten Minute Stop" [1936]
by Tennessee Williams

Acknowledgments and Thanks

First and foremost: **Donald Bain** and **Renée Paley-Bain** of Hyphenates Books for seeing this manuscript through to publication.

Robin Stockdale, who has been first editor for everything I ever wrote.

David Stockdale, my son, who is also a whiz of an editor.

Nathan Striedinger, my grandson of Gas City Records, LLC (www.gascityrecords.com), who designed the front cover.

Josh Rosenbaum, a musical genius who has been supportive and most helpful in musical suggestions, especially lyrics.

Chapter I

Thoughts of a terrorist attack had vanished from the minds of those who still had workable ones. The smog had somehow miraculously been driven away during the night by a strange and unexpected wind blowing off the Verdugo Mountain range, which cut across Our Lady, the Queen of the Angels of Porciuncula, known today simply as L.A. The result was an absolutely idyllic pristine Hollywood, and the sun had never shown so gloriously.

Because of this unexpected freeing of the atmosphere from vehicular carbon monoxide and other pollutants entrapped by the geographic position of the city, emphysemic old-timers with surgically enhanced faces in tight frozen smiles had been allowed to sit outside—albeit strapped in their wheelchairs, oxygen tanks at the ready—next to the green ceramic tiled pool at the assisted living nursing home, La Siesta Finale. Those who could whiled away their time in the early morning sun, reminding themselves why the great film studios had been built in Hollywood: because of glorious clear blue skies, sun and more sun!

A mile or so away stood the ten-foot medieval wrought-iron gates which guarded Lay RòthChîld Film Studios. Inside the tallest of the structures, surrounded by a New England-style village, was Wardrobe, a place where decades of costumes—those not stolen by the actors—had been carelessly hung on wire hangers. It had been only recently that Harry Roth discovered this sacrilege and had ordered his executive director Peter Katsen to do something about it.

Pittsburgh O'Casey was the expert hired to right the wrongs of years of sloth and neglect. Although he was a set dresser, known in the business as a "pillow plumper," he had studied historic costuming at Carnegie Tech with Miss Tess Whitte, a tough maiden lady, who thanks to her ferocious love of history and costuming forced all theatre students to memorize the various historic modes.

Thus Pittsburgh, a permanent fixture in the set dressers' union, was known as one of the studio's best, most exacting, and fastidious (indeed some called him a compulsive anal-retentive) workers. It was for these qualities that he was chosen by Mr. Katsen to inventory the studio's collection, catalogue each costume by historic period and store it in an air conditioned vault maintaining a sixty degree year-round temperature.

The job had turned out to be ten hours a day, seven days a week. With a heart condition and approaching the age of ninety-five, Studio Head Harry Roth had declared that he would not die until the job was finished. To this end, Katsen— normally a stickler for small economies—had urged Pittsburgh to hire three assistants. But by dint of experience and hard knocks, Pittsburgh had learned that he could not trust others to get the exact date of the historic mode of each garment, nor could he trust them to take the tender loving care necessary for such a job. In fact, exactness and love—along with curiosity about the stars who had worn these garments—had forced his decision: he would hire one assistant to take notes and a Polaroid snapshot of each costume, and he would do the rest. That way the job would be done right. Coming to work that morning at seven he was determined to get as much accomplished as possible.

"Oh, Lord have mercy!" he said, spying the moss green velvet in one of the racks of slovenly wedged-together costumes. "Do these eyes deceive or is this Scarlett's going-to-meet-Rhett gown?"

Rod, Pittsburgh's assistant—his real name was Percival but an agent had changed it—had bitterly resented being called so early on a Sunday morning. He was hung over, tired, bored and hungry, and it was only nine o'clock.

"What movie?" Rod asked through a yawn.

"Surely, you jest!" Pittsburgh said at the very moment he managed to extricate the moss-green velvet from the costumes surrounding it.

"Why would I 'jest' when I'm working my ass off inventorying this crap?" Rod snarled.

"Crap?" Pittsburgh asked incredulously. "The *Gone With The Wind* gown?"

"Jeez, I dint know."

It annoyed Pittsburgh to hear 'dint' for didn't. The speech teacher at Carnegie, Madam Ledith Minor—"speak with distinction," had been her cry throughout years of teaching—would have spun in her grave at such lazy-tongue, teeth, lips, and jaw diction.

Pittsburgh not only thought of himself as a tough cookie, he *was* a tough—albeit compassionate—cookie. Life had made him thus. He had no truck with, nor cottoned to, nor got all warm and runny when a hunk actor went into his little boy charmer pout. Miss Whitte—in her late fifties for well over two decades—was notoriously partial to hunks who sat splay-legged in the front row. Her not demanding the same professional standards from hunky actors as from their less well endowed fellow students was her one flaw.

But Pittsburgh would not think of that now. The gown was a find! Like the discovery of Marilyn's undies in Lee Strasberg's storage in an Upper West Side warehouse. Indeed, the excavation of Scarlett's going-to-meet-Rhett gown was to a costumer as important as the discovery of the Rosetta Stone to a scholar of hieroglyphs. He had been told—or legend had it—that the original costumes designed by Walter Plunkett had been given to the Producer's Collection at the University of Texas. But screw-ups were aplenty and there was undoubtedly a copy made; this might actually be the original. Holding the gown to his body, he looked in the mirror, scanning the fabric for possible dry rot. The hoops in the skirt were badly bent and slightly rusted and the velvet was crushed, but there were no holes.

"Look," Rod whined, "if you're gonna try every one on, we're never gonna finish."

"Oh, fiddle-de-dee!" Pittsburgh chided, humming the dance music from GWTW's ball scene as he danced across the room, holding the dress in front of him to see if the fabric still "moved."

"What year should I put down?" Rod asked.

"It's a hooped skirt from *Gone With The Wind*, for christsake!" Pittsburgh said. "What period do you think it's from, the Byzantine?"

"I don't know," Rod grumbled, adjusting the crotch of his jeans.

"Late 1850's, of course. Here, put it on the dummy and take the picture."

It was as he turned to extract another costume that he stumbled and almost lost his balance. Usually light on his feet, he could not understand what had happened. He thought of the moment in *Dark Victory* when Miss Bette Davis had her first blackout. But no, it wasn't his sight; he wasn't going blind; it was his balance. Could it be an Al-Qaeda attack against Hollywood?"

Did you feel anything?" he asked Rod.

In their laboratory on Mt. Palomar, just northeast of San Diego in the Cleveland National Forest, Rick Davis and Bill Burley, two California Institute of Technology seismologists, were in a heated discussion about the Oakland Raiders and the L.A. Dodgers when they felt the first tremor.

Glancing at the Richter Scale's fluttering needle, a chill went through Rick's body. Quickly calculating the subterranean origin, he concluded that the focus of the quake was the San Fernando fault, its epicenter at Lay RòthChîld Film Studios.

Bill immediately contacted the Tsunami Warning System and was informed that a series of movements caused by volcanic eruptions on the Pacific's floor had resulted in tsunami waves which were, at that very moment, traveling at speeds of up to 500 miles an hour toward The City of Angels.

Bill thought fleetingly of the destruction when an earthquake struck Lisbon, Portugal, in1755, and the Japanese tsunami of 2011, and he knew that as soon as the waves reached the shallow waters off the California coast they would slow, causing their length to shorten and their height to rise to a possible one hundred feet before they crashed upon the city.

∽⊙

Inside Wardrobe at Lay RòthChîld Film Studios, there was a tearing rent and the room's floor split down the geometric pattern of its mosaic parquet. Rod, on the crumbling side, screamed and held out a hand. Acting instinctively and grabbing onto the end of a permanently installed costume rack, Pittsburgh reached out. For a split second the light of hope lit up Rod's steely blue eyes as his body seemed suspended in space. Pittsburgh did the only thing he could. He snatched the gown from Rod's out-stretched hands just before the hunky assistant plummeted into the flaming abyss.

Drawing back in horror, he began to question his choice. But there was no time to think now. He would think about thinking tomorrow! Clutching the gown to his breast, he ran down the back stairs which, even as he ran, buckled beneath his feet.

Leaping nimbly over twisting steel, he ran toward his car. But as he approached, it became a fiery mass. In his mind's eye he envisioned Scarlett leaving a burning Atlanta and this image infused in him a determination to survive, just as she had survived, saving Melanie and the baby and driving back to Tara.

It was then that he saw the sign, LARGE PROPS. An outdoor storage area contained airplanes used in some of the studio's most famous films: *Ceiling Zero, The Wild Blue Yonder* and *Test Pilot* with Spencer Tracy and Clark Gable! Further along was a row of "jolly green giants" from *M*A*S*H, The Deer Hunter,* and *Apocalypse Now.* How fortuitous! Helicopters had the capability of rising vertically from the earth. A sudden eruption of water in the form of a geyser catapulted him into action. Props storage was surrounded by a ten-foot-high fence. Carefully tucking the gown inside his shirt, he grasped the wire mesh, and pulling his body upward secured a toehold.

Topping the fence was a spool of razor wire. The sharp teeth would lacerate his hands and he would never be able to properly plump a pillow again. But if that was the trade off for his life. . .

He was pondering this dilemma when he heard a horrendous burst of sound. Turning, he saw the black wrought-iron gates of Lay RòthChîld Film Studios writhe, camelback, tear apart and fling their imported Italian Renaissance devil-faced gargoyles into the air.

Galvanized into action, he scanned the top of the fence. Two posts set a foot and a half apart supported a copper-plated sign, written in Old English script, "Keep Out! Properties of Lay RòthChîld Film Studios." Where the posts connected—My God! Did he see correctly?—there was a break in the deadly razor wire.

Moving crab-like over the wire mesh, he heard explosions, one after another. Climbing upward toward the break in the razor wire, he thought of the carelessness of the security people. Had they run out of razor wire and intended to cover the cross bar at a later time? No, this was just one more example of the lack of pride in a job well done. What had happened to the Protestant work ethic?

Finding a secure foothold, he pushed upward, thrusting his torso over the cross-bar. Now balanced, he waited as gaseous black smoke engulfed him. In high school he had been mascot for the football team. Dressed in a black-and-orange striped tiger suit, papier-mâché head and cotton-stuffed tail, he was the one who had led—somersaulting and hand-springing—The Fighting Tigers onto the field. Hearing the roar of the crowd for the first time he had doubled the somersaults and-hand springs until the scantily attired Golden Girl majorette said, "Honey, save yourself. They're cheering for me and the team."

As he remembered things past, a telephone pole suddenly tore loose from a newly open chasm and fell, wires hissing and writhing across the concrete floor of the LARGE PROPS area.

Finding a higher foothold, and taking a deep breath, he pushed his thighs over the crossbar. But his body, prepared for a flying somersault so he would land on his feet, was halted precipitously in midair. Recovering from the brain loosening jolt and suspended upside down, he saw what had stopped him. The right leg of his trousers had caught the steel teeth of a dangling razor wire, attached itself to the strong twilled cotton, and was slowly ripping and lowering him. Could he wait to be lowered? The felled telephone pole's electric wires were snaking toward the fence. If they made contact he would be incinerated, just as Jimmy Cagney had been in *White Heat*, clinging to Sing Sing's prison fence.

Reaching up, he unzipped his fly, unbuckled his belt, slipped out of the penny loafers, and arched his feet to on-point and slid easily out of his trousers. But as he did so he felt a sudden sharp pain as the razor wire sliced into his right leg. A quick examination assured him that although messy, the wound was manageable. Tearing loose from the trousers, his eyes darted wildly over the area.

There was the airplane used by The Red Baron. Close to it was Lindy's The Spirit of St. Louis, and over there the plane that Amelia Earhart had used on her ill-fated flight. Still further was the Enola Gay, with the famous pretty girl pin-up of Lana Turner painted on its payload gates. And over there—it took his breath away—was the craft which had been used in *Thirty Seconds Over Tokyo* with Van Johnson, Spencer Tracy and the one and only Robert Mitchum!

But he must not tarry! Stepping into his trousers he flung himself into the first helicopter in line with its black control panel and felt his confidence shrivel. But then, as chance would have it, his eyes were drawn to the ignition. A careless prop person had failed to remove the keys.

Whataya gonna do? Props! He turned the key and heard the terrifying sound as the propeller blades slowly revved. Before him was the T-bar. Grasping it he closed his eyes and gently pulled. He felt the craft's nose tilt upward and raise into the air. When at last he dared look down, he saw Lay RòthChîld Film Studios, surrounded by flames and geysers, sliding—s l i d i n g—toward the sea.

As the craft gained altitude he looked out over the city of heartbreaks. But his view—rather like that of Griffith's famous balloon-shot from *Intolerance*—was not of Belshazzar's Feast but of Hollywood's Armageddon: burning, gyrating, splitting and being torn asunder, as by an angry god. Valentino's Moorish mansion "Falcon Lair," and—Oh God, the pain!—April East's "Ravenworld!" Both rubble. Further on, at Grauman's Chinese, the earth hurled the precious concrete slabs of stars' hand prints. Swanson's mansion with its all-black, onyx bathroom and Harold Lloyd's 45-room fortress "Greenacres" were crumbling.

Suddenly, the helicopter's windows steamed over, blocking his view. At the same time he felt an intense humidity. Turning on the windshield wipers, the slicing blades cleared the glass and he saw the hundred foot tsunami about to hit the fiery city.

Gaze one last time, an inner voice commanded, look upon the destruction of this cemetery of virtue with its hacienda door. A montage of celluloid royalty flashed through his mind: "Big Mack" Sennett, Fatty Arbuckle, Chaplin, Pola Negri, Monroe, Leigh, Davis, Crawford, and of course, the greatest of them all, April East, who had up to this point survived them all. "Goodnight sweet princess," he whispered, "and flights of angels sing thee to thy rest."

A conflagration of flames and exploding pulsating earth, rocked by the tsunami which, with unerring accuracy, had sliced loose the 34,000 square miles which constituted the five counties: Los Angeles, Orange, Riverside, San Bernardino, and Ventura, along with their population of 14.5 million and slowly—ever so slowly—washed them into the sea.

It may have been only a few minutes or an hour later when the helicopter began to slide earthward. Shaking himself from trauma-induced lethargy he looked at the gas gauge. The needle was on empty! The craft was falling just to the west of the fault but so close he could reach out and touch the newly formed cliff on the eastern side. Below, the sea roared in and covered the churning muddy wreckage.

Opening the door on the passenger side, he flung himself onto the cliff. Grasping the exposed roots from a eucalyptus tree, he pulled himself upward. Suspended for a moment, gasping for breath, he saw the ground around the roots begin to crumble. Gaining a toehold in the cliff's torn flesh and thrusting upward, he reached over the edge, grabbed the slender trunk of a sapling, and pulled himself slowly, inch by inch, praying to the blessed Saint Theresa until he lay panting and in utter exhaustion upon the ground. Then, sensing the danger of a cave-in, he rose, and clutching the moss green velvet inside his shirt, ran for thirty yards before he fell on *terra firma*.

How long he lay there he did not know, but later he would remember opening his eyes and looking west to see an extraordinarily beautiful sunset over the Pacific. But Hollywood was gone! He felt the awful ache of it, and with this realization, his fingers dug into the soft earth. Lifting a piece of loosened sod heavenward he cried out, "As God is my witness, I will do everything I can to save the legend!"

And then he fainted.

Chapter II

Nick—whose full name was Nicola Battisti Andreotti Sabbatini, straight, smart, thirty-something with drop-dead good looks—arrived at the Don's mansion in Brooklyn at 12:55. He hated getting up early on a Sunday when the only people on the streets were the out-of-towners and health nuts headed to the park. He much preferred lazy late Sunday morning sex with Suzie.

The early-rising Don, however, wished the tutoring session to start promptly at one p.m. and Nick was taught by his father that when the leader of an organized crime family says "immediatamente," he means it.

Sundays were the Don's special time. Celebration of the Eucharist was no problem since he attended the shorter, 5 o'clock drunkard's mass on Saturday. The Sabbath was reserved for sitting in his red leather overstuffed fold-out chair, crucifix on the wall behind him, listening to his favorite composer, Giacomo Puccini.

Today it was *Suor Angelica* with Lucia Popp.

The story of Angelica's redemption after giving birth to an illegitimate child was exactly what he needed. He recently had ordered the cement-booted, off-the-Queensboro-Bridge-and-into-the-East-River drowning of several disloyal members of the family; the story of Sister Angelica and God's compassion, backed as it was by celestial music, was reassuring.

In the living room he heard Nick, in a perfect Bolognese accent, say for what must have been the hundredth time, "buon giorno," and his only child, a daughter, Madonna Corleone, cursed with a lateral lisp which made speaking the Italian language—one of the most liquid and beautiful sounds on earth—virtually impossible, repeating, "bun yern o."

A freshman at The Borough of Manhattan College on Chambers Street, Madonna was taking Italian as her foreign language requirement for the two-year Associate's degree, and was failing the course. The Don had hired Nick to tutor her. A patient tutor, he once again clearly articulated the greeting "buon giorno," and over a high note sung by Lucia Popp, the Don crossed himself as he heard his daughter reply, "bun yern o."

In a small, fourth floor apartment in an old brownstone on 76th street on Manhattan's Upper West Side, Suzie Miller, an intelligent and beautiful twenty-five year old brunette, had just finished dialing the Brooklyn number.

Before her on the television screen was the President of the United States.

"My fellow Citizens, let us mark this catastrophe by remembering who we are and what we have always stood for. In the year of our country's birth, with winter's icy grip upon their throats, our patriot forefathers, huddled by an icy river . . ."

The phone rang several times in the Mafia mansion.

In the kitchen, Mrs. Don, a woman less than five feet in height, with breasts so heavy she perpetually tilted forward, prepared her husband's mid-afternoon dinner. She was in the final stage of cooking the pasta's sauce, which bubbled in the large iron caldron and had reached that most delicate stage when oregano had to be introduced. "Mamma mia," she uttered under her breath on the fifth ring, "Chi è? Ma va fan' culo!" Opening the kitchen door, she howled, "Il telefono!"

The Don crossed himself, got up, and picked up the receiver. "Pronto," he said in a voice that sounded hoarse.

"Sorry to bother you but I need to speak to Nick Sabbatini." Even while Suzie was speaking the President was saying, "...the very warmth from their campfires replaced by charred remains . . ."

"Attenda, prego." Moving to the sliding oak doors into the living room the Don called, "Scusi, Signor Sabbatini. Al telefono!"

"Il telefono, for me?" Nick asked.

The Don shook his head. "Si, si."

"Scusi," Nick said to Madonna.

"Thi, thi, Thin yoray," she lisped

"Grazie," he said to the Don as he entered the study.

"Prego," the Don answered, indicating the phone.

"Hello?"

"Nick, sorry to bother you at work," Suzie said.

The Don, who had settled back comfortably in his chair, turned down the CD player's volume.

"What is it?" Nick asked.

"Have you heard the news?" Suzie asked.

"What news?"

"The Big One hit California."

"The Big One?"

"A ten on the Richter scale."

"My God!"

The Don's attention now shifted from the opera to the conversation. "California's been hit by a bad quake," Nick told him.

"I'm watching the report right now," Suzie said. "Listen . . . ." She held the phone toward the TV.

"George Washington said to his troops, 'Let it be told that in this winter of our discontent, with nothing but our hope and virtue . . .'"

The Don had turned on the television with his remote so Nick was not sure if he was hearing Suzie's TV or the one in the

Don's library. ". . . that our Shining City on the Hill, armed by our common dangers, came forth to meet them when in a day of infamy our beloved Hollywood sank into the sea . . ."

"My God! Hollywood gone!" Nick gasped.

"Vanished! It was the tsunami," Suzie explained, "Listen."

"With only virtue and hope remaining, our forefathers faced a disaster there on the wintery Potomac. Let us follow their example. Let it be known by our children, and our children's children and our grandchildren and great grand-children and beyond into the hundredth generation of Americans that when we were tried and tested by the great tsunami, just as our forefathers before us were tried and tested over and over again, that with God's grace upon us we picked ourselves up, dried ourselves off, and with the unique courage and determination that has marked our nation, we shall start—hear me—we *shall* start, we shall start, we shall start all over again."

✧

It was the next morning that Suzie, dressed and ready for work, leaned over the Castro convertible and kissed the heavily stubbled Nick, who'd had a very bad night. "Darling," she said, "try not to think about it."

"Hollywood, gone," he said for the thousandth time. "I can't believe it."

"Why don't you rent a couple of movies today."

Nick brightened. "Good call," he said. "I'll stream some of the early April East films and make today kind of a memorial."

"You do that, darling," Suzie said.

"And remember," Nick called after her, "try to find something—anything! I can't go on tutoring Madonna."

"Darling, it's not her fault that she's clef-palate challenged. But I will check the want-ads in the *Times*."

"Maybe Mr. Jukes could help. You said he was from a very old and. . ."

". . . *inbred*, New York family. The Jukes are famous because of the eugenics movement."

"Love you," Nick called.

"Love you," Suzie said as she closed the door.

On a cliff overlooking the Pacific, Pittsburgh was awakened by what sounded like hammering. Gaining consciousness he saw a man pounding a 'For Sale, Beach Property' sign into the ground. So soon after the tragedy? He could not believe his eyes. Shaking his head in an attempt to rid his sight of the vision, he looked out over the ocean where there were dozens of surfers.

Suzie Miller was not only beautiful, she was an uncommonly good person. Hurrying down Columbus Avenue she give a dollar to a homeless man just outside their lone neighborhood bank. Further on she signed, "top of the morning to you" to an Irish deaf mute. And in the next block she dropped all the change she had into the turned-up cap atop the baby grand on which the one-armed Juilliard student played classical music. The flag was at half staff at the Columbus Circle office building where she worked and long black banners were draped through its parapets. Racing across the lobby, she managed to crowd into a Muzak-playing, limited-stops elevator.

Extracting herself at the 49th floor's Media Entertainment Division, she was retina-scanned while a security dog sniffed her bag. When she heard the phone, a glance at her watch told her it was only five minutes to ten; still the call might be important. "Good morning, Milkin/Bush, Media Entertainment Division."

"Lemme speak to Harry."

The voice was sultry, sensual, voluptuously husky.

"May I say who's calling?" Suzie asked.

"Honey, you gotta be kiddin' me. Either that or you wuz born yesterday. This is April East."

Suzie almost dropped the receiver. "*Ms.* East?" she gasped.

"You got it, Toots!"

"But I th . . . th . . . thought . . ."

"That I'd expired in the quake? Nah, I got a feeling somethin' was gonna shake and I knew it wasn't me, so I caught the red-eye and skipped the light fantastic outta town."

"Oh, thank God you're safe!"

"God had nothin' to do with it, kiddo. Now, how's about puttin' Harry on the horn?"

Suzie glanced quickly into the open door of CEO Harry Jukes's office. It was empty. He had probably gone to the men's room. "I'm afraid Mr. Jukes isn't at his desk right now, Ms. East. Is there anything *I* can do?"

"From the sound of your voice, honey, I figure you're a dame. I like cowboys."

"Mr. Jukes will be devastated to have missed your call. Is there any message?"

"Look, kid, tell 'im for me, I've been listenin' to the Prez on the boob tube and I'm thinkin' of maybe makin' a comeback, doin' one of those MTV videos for the Hollywood Disaster Relief Fund like that thing they did for Haiti a few years back."

"*We Are The World* for the starving children of Haiti?" Suzie asked.

"Yeah, and I was wonderin' if Harry'd wanta produce."

In the Milkin/Bush board room, gathered around a long oval table made from the trunk of one of the famous northern California redwoods just after the "Hug a Tree" bill was passed by Congress during W's Administration, were seated lawyers and members of the Executive Committee on Entertainment exulting over the April East bonanza. It had been a long afternoon discussing dramatic, musical, TV, foreign, print and film rights from the sale or licensing of "the property" which included "without limitation" the plot, themes, title, characters, copyright, and adaptations. The discussion was now down to ancillaries: spin-offs, T-shirts, sneakers, comic books, intergalactic exports, followed by a probable release date, billing credits and last, who they would hire to direct. The names of Sir Peter Jackson, Clint Eastwood, Sofia Coppola, Michael Moore, and Joe Mantello were all mentioned and quickly dropped since they knew that hiring a director was the least of their worries.

Mohammad, the richest of the executives, an Oxonian, attired splendidly in his native Saudi garb, spoke for the first time. "Might I suggest, not a specific person, but the *kind* of director needed."

"Shoot," Harry said.

"Someone very *now*."

"Howdaya mean, Mo?"

"Well, I'd say someone who's a. . . a . . . post-*post*-modernist deconstructionist minimalist." Mohammad paused for the words of his Harvard undergraduate education to sink in. "Perhaps even—dare we be so bold—a neo-Italian realist."

"I'll buy that, Mo." Harry put one thumb up to signify agreement.

It was then that Suzie did something she had never before done at an executive meeting. She raised her hand. "Excuse me," she said, "may I make a suggestion?"

Working late that evening, she had typed the minutes of the meeting into the computer and then rushed home. At the 76th Street brownstone she checked her mailbox in the small foyer, looked both ways before unlocking the inside door, and ran up the four flights, pausing to check the hallway on each floor before arriving at the apartment. She heard the television blaring inside. Removing two keys from her tightly clutched strap bag, she unlocked the door and entered.

An unshaven Nick, in boxers, was propped up on the unmade Castro, black armband around his left bicep, watching a flick.

"You'll never guess who called today," she sang out.

Nick held up his hand for silence. "Shhhh," he said reverently. "It'll be over in a minute." Wearing chain mail cut to reveal her cleavage April East stood before the evil French Tribunal, a burning pyre of fagots behind her, and raised her sword in victory. As the wavering recorded music reached its climax, "The End" flashed across the screen.

"Is that it?" Suzie asked.

"Sure," Nick said, clicking rewind.

"But Joan of Arc was burned at the stake."

"East changed the ending," Nick said.

"Changed history?"

"The difference between history and a movie is that history tells what actually happened and a film what could happen. So a film is more important— philosophically speaking—than history."

"Oh," Suzie said, although what he said did not sound quite right.

Having watched the scantily attired East all day, an aroused Nick pulled Suzie down on the Castro and began to nibble her ear. His hand reached into her blouse and his breathing became more pronounced as he whispered, "You were saying?"

"When?"

"When you came in."

"That you'd never guess who called. I think you may be up for a film job."

Nick sat upright. "Whataya mean?"

"It was a call from Miss East?"

"She's still alive!"

"Yes, she left Hollywood at midnight, apparently after having a presentiment."

"She's in town?"

"She owns that brownstone on 49th just off 2nd, in the same block where Hepburn and Sondheim lived."

"She made it out alive?"

"Yes."

"Way to go!" Nick let out a whoop.

After he'd settled down, Suzie told him how the office had been thrown into total chaos and how Mr. Jukes had called Miss East and told her he'd be honored to produce her *We Are The Survivors* video for the benefit of the HDRF.

"HDRF?"

"The Hollywood Disaster Relief Fund. It was when Sheikh Mohammad AttaZar put forth his idea of a neo-Italian minimalist that I told Mr. Jukes about you."

"But," Nick gasped, "no one's ever heard of me."

"What difference does that make? The committee members don't know anything about directors."

"But, my God! A star of April East's magnitude—making a comeback—with *me* as director?"

"Well, no one ever directs her. She does that herself. And of course she must be very old," Suzie said.

"How did she sound over the phone?"

"Kinda sexy."

"There, you see?"

"But her voice is one thing, her face and body may have . . ."

"Gloria Swanson, born in 1899, married six times plus boffing Joe Kennedy all those years. Marlene Dietrich was born in 1900 and what about Lena Horne, born in 1917. Has East aged at all?"

"Well, I'll admit she looked terrific just now in that last scene of *Maid of Orleans* but. . ."

"*Made in Orleans*" Nick corrected her. "I'd be willing to bet she's still got gorgeous breasts. Oh, yeah! And the way she parts her lips and opens her eyes wide when she looks up at you, all anyone can think of . . . "

"And she could have had her face lifted," Suzie said.

"Ruth Gordon never had her face lifted. She did facial exercises to keep the skin tight. Swanson and Dietrich dieted. Even in the

best of restaurants they carried their own health food. All of those
broads stayed out of the sun. And as long as April East is still
around, I'll bet she's kept herself young. She's a myth, a legend, an
American icon!"

"Well, of course getting to direct is just a possibility."

Nick was beginning to cotton to the idea. "Me direct April
East. Maybe I could get my old buddy from school, Dean, to work
as a . . ."

"Cinematographer. He's not doing anything, is he?"

"No. We've only been out of school a few years and . . . It takes
time."

"So if he could handle the camera stuff."

"Yeah. He's the best handheld cameraman in the business. But,
of course, I've got so little experience."

"Look," Suzie said. "You majored in Italian at the University of
Indiana. You spent three years at the University of Bologna on your
Junior year abroad."

Nick heard the Don's daughter saying "bun yern o" over and
over again: a voice-over with echo-chamber enhancements.

"And you've got your MFA at N.Y.U. and you've *seen* every film
April East ever made about a hundred times, plus practically every
other film ever made. You've read every book on films that was ever
published and with a little help . . .Look, Nick," she said, getting
down to brass tacks, "the Don owes you. I mean, seeing to it that
you got through school was good, but this tutoring job for a measly
two hundred bucks a week?"

"It's only for two hour's work," Nick said.

"Still, that's hardly 'looking after you.' After all it was your
father who took the hit. . . ."

⤳⤳

Even though it was past his bed time, his father had allowed Nick
to go with him to have dinner with the Don. He remembered the
little suit and tie, his mother greasing his hair and dabbing on

some of his father's lilac aftershave, and his father leading him proudly into the midtown Italian restaurant.

The concertina player sang "O Solo Mio" while strong men paid court at their table, kissing both the Don and his father on both cheeks and on the lips, and chucking Nick under the chin.

What camaraderie! And the red-checked tablecloths and the flame from the candle stuck in a Chianti bottle and the pumpkin ravioli and his father letting him take a sip of the *vino rosso della casa*, and afterwards the *gelato al pistacchio* and . . . and then leaving the restaurant followed by the Don . . . and then . . . the horror!

The Don's bodyguard had just opened the door of the stretch black limousine when he heard a scream of tires and a car rounded the corner, four men in raincoats and George Raft hats on its running boards. Springing into action, his father threw himself in front of the Don, as the hideous rat-tat-tat of the machine guns made his father's body contract like a rag doll. And then the yelling, the commotion and confusion and people running from the restaurant and the blood oozing through his father's white shirt and Nick bending over crying, "Daddy, Daddy," and his father saying to the Don, who was holding his bullet-riddled body like Mary holding Jesus in the Pieta, "Minimo, take care of . . . my boy . . . Nick," and the Don, tears welling up in his eyes, saying, "Massimo, I swear on the grave of my mother, I'll look after your Nick." And then Nick's father died in the Don's arms . . . .

After a moment to let Nick clear his head of the remembrance of this childhood tragedy, Suzie asked, "Are you certain the car had a running board?"

"Sure I'm sure, why?"

"Because, darling, they stopped building cars with running boards before you were born."

"Well, maybe I was thinking. . ."

". . .of a scene from a movie?"

Nick nodded.

"Anyway, as I was saying, the Don owes you."

"How could he help?" Nick asked.

"Well, goodness, how do you think Milkin/Bush is financed? Oh, Nick don't be so naive! It's Mafia connected, Hon."

Maybe Suzie was right, he thought. She usually was. Maybe he should go to Brooklyn and ask the Don if he could help. But he hated the long subway ride, and after watching April East's gorgeous breasts and swaying ample hips all afternoon he was horny as hell.

"Well," Suzie smiled, checking his boxers, "Call the Don later."

It was the next morning that Suzie received the call. As soon as she heard the voice she knew who it was. "One moment, please," she said and pressed the button on the intercom.

Harry Jukes picked up the phone as Suzie covered the receiver with her hand and listened in on the conversation.

She heard the Don's hoarse voice, "Harry, do me a favor . . ."

"Anything!"

"Nicola Battisti Andreotti Sabbatini . . . a good Italian boy. Very talented. You remember the name?"

"Yes! Yes!" Harry said. "His name came up only yesterday at the board meeting as a possible director."

"Hire him!"

Chapter III

A month after The Big One, hunk hardhat Hank Hendricks, a 23-year-old construction worker, was at work on the new 150-story Palson/Trump skyscraper going up across from Grand Central Station.

When he had arrived that morning, he noted an unusual amount of activity: some 20 satellite and microwave vans on the street, reporters working their Blackberries, and camera crews milling around on 42nd Street and Vanderbilt Avenue. He figured it for a film shoot or a celebrity coming from out of town.

It was later, while he was walking a girder, that a flurry of activity caused him to look down.

From the West Side came a full-siren NYPD escort of several cars with rotating flashers followed by a black stretch limo. Hank's first thought was that the President was going to be speaking at the U.N., which meant traffic would be screwed up all day. But the limo hung a U, pulled up in front of the station and a uniformed chauffeur hopped out and opened the door.

She was wearing a low cut dress, feather boa around her neck, and black picture hat with ostrich feathers, which she removed revealing her red hair. Hot Ziggety! A red-haired bombshell with a slim waist, curvy hips and cheeky butt. "Get a load of those bazooms!" he said to Dizzy, who was working the same girder.

Dizzy looked down, bugged his eyes and then grabbing his crotch thrust his tongue rapidly in and out as Hank let out a low wolf whistle.

The redhead looked up, but instead of shaking her fists, she swayed her hips, locked eyes with him and waved.

"Baby," Hank called down, "Don't do me this way!"

She cupped her hand at the back of her ear.

"You're lightin' my fire in a hard hat zone!" he yelled.

She moved the tip of her tongue around her lips and blew him a kiss. By this time she had the attention of the entire girder gang and they went wild.

Dizzy, an old-timer with a face like a leather pouch, suddenly stopped lapping his tongue in and out and yelled, "Holey Moley! It's April East!" Her name was repeated again and again in a ripple effect like a rock hurled into water, until every man on the steel girders knew who was standing below. She had been made famous by the cartoonist, Norse of Norway, who immortalized her in a series of adult pornographic animations on DVD and in comic books. There wasn't a Joe-six-pack on a girder who hadn't gotten a sweaty adolescent boner and whacked off looking at a naked April East in all manner of positions. Camera crews were now in action as a cordon of New York's finest sprang from rotating-red-light patrol cars and formed a protective ring around the sex goddess. Pandemonium erupted on the street. Traffic was brought to a standstill. Jaded New York commuters, intent on getting to the office, who wouldn't have stopped had J.C. himself appeared skate boarding down 42nd Street, bunched together and gaped. Overhead, building constructors banged their plastic hard hats against steel beams, fondled their genitals, imitated howling wolves, and some hung upside down from the girders.

On the pretext of fixing her stockings, she suddenly bent over revealing the outline of her butt. Bending her knees, turning her body, wiggling her ass, putting her hands in the air, on her hips, on her thighs, she thrust out her pelvis, puckered up her lips, opened her mouth and blew kisses as the cameramen zoomed in, flashes exploding.

It was during this photo op session, unnoticed by anyone, that a veiled figure in black moved into the ticketed passenger's waiting room overlooking Grand Central's main hall to watch the show.

‿כ

Trailed by her black maid, April made her way languidly down the ramp and turned right at the Bakery Basket into Grand Central's main concourse.

To the degree that women were offended by East's open promotion of sexual aggression in the male, African Americans were equally offended by her 'colored maid,' and at that very moment 500 of them were marching across Brooklyn Bridge toward City Hall.

Beulah The Second—there had been a Beulah before her—was dressed in an exact imitation of the actress Hattie McDaniel who played "Mammy" in *Gone With The Wind*, to whom she bore a striking resemblance. She now waddled several paces behind her mistress, red-bandanna-ed, dressed in a floor length skirt, a white apron, tight blouse which imprisoned her enormous breasts, and long sleeves that covered her heavy arms. To further emphasize the stereotype, she carried a worn carpetbag, shook her head, and looked disapprovingly as her mistress made playful sexual banter with New York's finest.

The star was surrounded by a ring of policemen. There was not a policewoman in sight. Ahead, at the side, behind, and standing on the roof of the information booth in the center of the terminal, the paparazzi, T.V. camera crews, technicians, tourists, and early morning rush hour commuters took it all in.

As April East received adulation inside the station, a cab pulled up near the Vanderbilt entrance and a middle-aged woman and a boy in a Buster Brown suit got out and waited for the driver to unload the luggage, which he tossed carelessly onto the sidewalk.

The woman paid him the twelve seventy-five fare, tucked the smaller bag under an arm, lifted the two heavier ones, and giving a nod for the boy to follow made her way toward the door, ignoring the cabby's curses.

A second yellow cab, unable to make it through traffic, pulled up at the side of the New York Public Library on 42nd Street between Sixth and Fifth, and four muscular young men slinging strap-bags over their shoulders pushed their way through the crowds. A third cab, stopping on the station's Park Avenue side, disgorged brunette Suzie Miller, Nick Sabbatini, and a young pianist, Rimsky Horowitz.

Chapter IV

In the basement Maplewood paneled recreation room of her home in Sandusky, Ohio, an angry octogenarian, Eunice Unger, sat on her Early American Maplewood vinyl sofa watching television with her husband. Joe had been channel surfing and had finally settled on CNN, claiming they gave more "in-depth" coverage to the East story.

Joe had been glued to the tube ever since the story broke that April East was making a video for HDRF. Exactly how it would profit any of those who died when the tsunami hit LA was not stated in their "in-depth" report; no one knew anything about it even though oversights had supposedly been installed after the AIG executives received million-dollar bonuses paid with taxpayers' money from the President's stimulus package.

The East story received more coverage than the Guyana massacre, David Koresh's Branch Davidians, O.J. Simpson, Princess Diana, 9/11, Katrina, both the 2008 and 2012 elections, or the Casey Anthony or George Zimmerman-Trayvon Martin court cases. The East story had everything: tragedy, pathos, clamor, suspense, plus a D cup *heroine*. When it broke it wiped the main focus—The Big One—right off the map, and journalistic hyperbole elevated East to "the first and finest of Hollywood."

There followed retrospectives of April East's old films and television specials, on Max, her chauffeur, her dancing/musclemen back-ups, and re-runs of the death of Beulah the First. Eunice read that the East comeback was selling more commercials—Viagra probably—than any news story in TV history.

Her private railroad car, taken out of the moth ball fleet, had been attached to the Amtrak caboose when it left Grand Central Station. There was no mention, of course, that Amtrak was federally subsidized and was towing this private railroad car at taxpayers' expense.

Shots of the train departing included the sound of an old fashioned train whistle.

"Well, there you have it!" Eunice said in disgust. "Diesels don't have whistles." But before she could finish, there was a picture of a fat old Amtrak engineer saying he'd rigged up a tape and loud speakers so the train would *sound* like trains used to sound. "You know, that lonesome cry in the night." And when an interviewer asked why he'd done it, he said, "To comfort Miss East." In the background was a voiceover of Hank Williams singing:

"Hear that lonesome whippoorwill?
He sounds too blue to fly
The midnight train is whining low
I'm so lonesome, I could cry."

Well, it was a show! And like the Romans said, "Give the plebs a little bread and circus and they're as contented as a horse fly in a shithouse." The paparazzi went so far as to compare this train trip out to North Dakota to the one that took Abraham Lincoln's body from Springfield back to Washington for its final resting place under forty tons of cement.

At the first stop, Poughkeepsie, there was a picture of April East on the bunting-draped caboose, blowing kisses to the throngs— mostly men—gathered at the station. Next day, an official member of the press corps traveling on the train did a day- long series of interviews at various whistle stops. The first one was in a corn field. April East, dressed in cut-offs, a scythe in hand, posed with farmers on their John Deere-Mitsubishi tractors. Then at some hick burg in Indiana, dressed in cut-off striped denim bib overalls and clasping a brawny farm boy, she asked, "Whataya do, Ace?"

"I'm a farmhand."

"I'd sure trust you to plow my back forty!"

And then one of the shoulder straps on her coveralls broke. Lord help us! "Costume malfunction!" was the spin the press gave it, but it's a damn good thing that no one was standing in the way. They could've been smothered.

In Gary, Indiana where one pathetic steel mill had just reopened with bailout money, wearing a welder's hard hat and a blue work shirt unbuttoned halfway down, she posed while measuring the biceps of a young factory worker.

"I go for men of steel," she lisped, an obvious suck-up to the steel mill lobby, but the roar that went up from those factory hard-hats was mind-boggling.

Chapter V

Toward evening, the Amtrak pulled into Bismarck. April East's private railroad car was unhooked, backed onto a dead end siding, and the Amtrak continued on its way with a final farewell cry of its stereophonic lonesome whistle.

Her Packard, shipped in advance on a flatcar, immediately pulled alongside and April and Beulah were driven away while the exhausted television crews headed to the nearest watering hole.

Halfway through the back streets, East's driver, dressed in a leather jacket, jodhpurs, a visored cap and carrying a riding crop, stopped to study a map. As the car idled, a tumbleweed blew through the deserted street and lodged against the front wheel.

"Is there a problem, Max?" April asked.

"Madam," Max answered in his thick German accent. "I am checking to see if ve are headed in ze richt direction, ja vohl?"

"Yeah," April answered. "Vo."

"Was ich nicht weiss macht mich nicht heiss," Max hissed.

Out the window, April East saw the faded on-again-off-again letters of the neon sign, BAR and a young Brad Pitt type lounging languidly against the cement block building.

"Roll down the window, Max," she ordered.

"Was man nicht kann meiden muss man wilig leiden," Max said, pressing the control.

"Hey, kid!" she called. "Could you tell us how to get to Timbuckone?"

The boy-toy removed a straw from his mouth and sauntered toward the Packard. "It's upstate in the boonies."

April crotch-cruised the tight packaged trousers and contemplated an overnight in Bismarck.

"Don't even think about it!" Beulah said.

"Well, as much as I hate to leave a swingin' place like Bismarck, my business is upstate," she said to the kid who was bent down at the window, eyeballing her cleavage.

"Wow! Ain't you . . . ? Didn't I see you on TV?"

"You got it, Cowboy."

The boy became suddenly shy. "Go straight till you get on 83 North," he stammered.

"And?" she prompted.

Swallowing hard, he continued. "At Wilton, turn right on 41 which turns left. Go north through Russo. Timbuckone's half way between Russo and Velva."

"Thanks, Sport," April said, and Beulah ordered Max to roll up the window, cutting off the sexual sparks emanating from her mistress.

If one could have observed, as in a balloon shot, highway 83 heading north, one would have seen not only the boonies through which the Packard moved, but three Bismarck taxis and a truck—which carried the star's gowns and personal paraphernalia—following at a respectful distance.

In the first taxi was a blond woman and the man-child, in the second the four male dancers, and in the third accompanist Rimsky Horowitz, along with Suzie and Nick. Several miles behind this entourage was a black stretch limo in which sat a lone figure in black.

The lead car pulled into Timbuckone at eleven p.m.

"Stop in front of the theatre, Max," April ordered.

"Ja vohl," Max growled, then under his breath muttered, "Zwischen Freud und Lied ist die Brücke nicht weit."

It was April who had insisted on using the Bijou for the location shot. Harry Jukes had wanted to use the old Victory Theatre on 42nd Street, but East, who still owned Timbuckone's Bijou, was adamant.

Built in the Greek Revival style, it was elegantly and elaborately ornate, although what had once made an impression of licentious and profligate luxury had now badly deteriorated. But the building had suffered through only two changes: from "legit" to motion pictures, closing with the advent of television, whereas New York's Victory had a long and agonizing descent into decay, burlesque, a grind house, and porn. Viewing the structure now by moonlight through the tinted vita-glass of the Packard, April turned to Beulah. "You think the goddamn place is safe?"

"You wouldn't've picked it if it wasn't," Beulah said.

Inside the taxi that pulled up just behind the Packard, the man-child looked out the window at the crumbling colonnade of the old theatre's portico and recalled a scene many years ago when the Bijou was in its splendor . . . .

The premiere of the silent film, *A Chicken In Every Pot*, was taking place, with the President of the United States and his wife in attendance. A swaying April East, in a fringed-leather outfit, sombrero, low-cut denim blouse, chaps and cowboy boots, sauntered down the aisle on the arm of her leading man, a swarthy, wavy-haired Latin Lover.

A pubescent J.O. North, Jr. with raging out-of-control hormones sat with Beulah The First in a box, screened off from the audience's view. He moved forward, resting one arm on the very edge of the box in order to get a better look at the handsome actor. Pulling him back roughly, Beulah warned, "Boy, you know you ain't suppose to be seen . . . ."

೧ಾ

The Packard pulled up at the entrance of the Bismarck. The hotel
was named for the German Chancellor so admired by J.O. North,
Sr. It was Timbuckone's tallest building, its seven stories towering
over the rest of the town. Built at the same time as the Bijou, its
top floor had been designed—no expense spared—as a luxury
apartment which was part of the bait by which the old man hoped
to lure his child bride back home.

In front of its crumbling facade, crowds of locals stood
respectfully on either side of the sawhorse partitioning off the
runway, which was covered with a faded red carpet. At the very
center stood Pittsburgh O'Casey.

As the Packard came into view, the high school band struck up
the military marching version of "For He's A Jolly Good Fellow."
The car stopped, Max opened the door, and April East stepped out
to the roar of the crowd.

The Mayor came forward. "Welcome, home, Miss East."

"Thanks, Mayor."

A child thrust a bouquet of roses into the air. April knelt, kissed the
child on the cheek, thanked her, and with one arm wrapped around
her, the other holding the bouquet, signaled that she was ready for the
photo-op. When the cameras were winding down, she said, "Thanks
again, darling," to the little girl, rose without the Mayor's awkward
attempts to help, and swept toward the hotel's lobby.

೧ಾ

As April East passed, Pittsburgh genuflected, a response which he
could only attribute to his Catholic upbringing. He simply could
not move. He had followed the television news reports whenever
he was not at work in the Bijou or at her apartment in the hotel,
and was aware of every moment of her progress across country. But
now that he had seen her in the flesh, was close enough to have
reached out and touched the hem of her gown, he was in a state
of euphoria.

⌒ⱺ

Inside the lobby, the star moved through vestiges of former grandeur: marble floors, red velvet drapes at ceiling-high windows, potted palms, and a splashing fountain representing the springs of Castalia with water ejecting from the mouth of a fig-leafed shepherd boy. The venerable hotel manager, in moth-eaten black tails, hobbled forward, bowing. "Welcome home, Miss East," he croaked.

"Hello, Pops," she said in her husky voice. "You ain't changed a bit!"

"I'm afraid I have," he said. "But you look younger than ever. What is it? Have you discovered Ponce de Leon's spring?"

"No, I ain't had a drink from the fountain of youth, Pops," she purred. "I just keep usin' it. Remember, Baby, if you don't use it, you lose it." She nudged him with her elbow, and as the old man cackled appreciatively her eyes seemed to be searching the lobby. "Where . . ." she asked, "where is the . . ."

"The elevator?"

"Yes."

"Right there," he pointed. "Right there where it's always been."

She moved quickly to the open, iron-barred cage. As it creaked slowly upward, taking its mistress to her seventh floor suite, the sharp iron spikes attached to its underside became visible.

⌒ⱺ

Pittsburgh, attempting to live forever in the moment, was brought back to reality when the taxi, which had waited patiently for the greeting ceremony and entrance of Miss East into the hotel, drove up. When the blond woman got out, he gasped, and as she was about to unload luggage he shrieked, "Mona!"

She turned. "Pittsburgh!" and the two ran and fell into each other's arms.

"Mona ala Mode!"

"Let me get a look at you," she said, holding him at arm's length. "Ain't you a sight for sore eyes?"

"And you look like always."

"And you haven't changed a bit." Mona laughed.

"God love you for a liar," Pittsburgh said in his Blanche DuBois imitation.

". . . daylight never exposed . . ." Mona added.

". . . so total a ruin," they said in unison before going into a synchronized Polish-peasant-routine followed by spitting in their palms and high-fiving.

After their laughter, Pittsburgh asked, "How long has it been?"

"We haven't worked a gig together for . . ."

The honking drew her attention. "Oh, look, I'm holding things up. Hold on a sec." She ran to the taxi, told the driver just to stack the luggage on the curb, and said to the boy, "Now just give me a moment, dear. Make yourself comfortable."

"How?" he demanded angrily.

"Please sit on the luggage and wait a moment. I'll be right with you."

Turning, she took Pittsburgh's arm and hurriedly drew him aside. "Look, Luv, this has gotta be fast. I'm in a crazy situation here. I contracted as her dresser and yes, I did agree to the 'availability for all assignments, as needed' clause. Yesterday morning, when I thought I was to accompany her on the trip, Aunt Jemima, that piece of shit, seemed to be the one running the show. She told me the weirdo and I would be traveling separately in a compartment in another part of the train and that I was not to leave it or allow him to leave, not even for the food that was already arranged for. I took one look and was about to tell her to shove the job where the sun don't shine but with the recession and work so scarce and, well, I gotta be honest. . ." She glanced back at the boy and lowered her voice to a whisper. "Their people ran a security check and found out I got fired from a job three years ago, and they talked to Zazloff, the new union boss, and he said if I gave them any trouble, he'd see that I never got another job. She's got power. And with the economy and all. . . ."

The second taxi in line drove up and out stepped four heavily muscled and handsome young men. "Wait just a sec. Who are those guys?" Pittsburgh asked. "The dancers?"

Mona nodded.

"Why so many flavors?"

"It was her idea."

As Mona hurried on, Pittsburgh could not help but notice Beulah watching them from the shadow of one of the colonnades. An African-American, Chinese-Asian-American, Spanish-Mexican-American, and a Caucasian, representing the "ethnic spectrum" of those lost in the quake. At least that's what *The Post* said.

"Where's J.O?" Beulah asked in a menacing voice as she stepped from behind the colonnade.

"He's resting for a second. I just met an old friend," Mona indicated Pittsburgh.

Beulah ignored him and called, "Mistuh J.O, you come wid me, boy!" And as the man-child rapidly complied, she jerked his arm and told Mona. "And you! Don't be long!"

"I'll get the bellhop to bring these up," Mona said, then added, *sotto voce* to Pittsburgh, "We got to talk so I can fill you in. Ta ta, Luv."

"Come over early in the morning and take a look at the set," Pittsburgh called after her. Something was totally off key and he was worried about her, but she had always been excitable, even back at school where they first met. Maybe the situation wasn't as bad as she indicated. As he was thinking about it, a third taxi arrived and two men and a young brunette woman got out. Who were they? With all the goings-on, he could not go up to his room yet. There was too much to think about. The truck with her costumes should be arriving soon, which he would offer to help unload. As he turned to leave, a car pulled up.

"Thanks for the lift, Mister, I appreciate your picking me up."

"No problem."

A Chinese-American stepped out and as the car drove away, the hitchhiker turned and saw Pittsburgh. "This is where Miss East's party is staying?"

"But . . . I saw you go in!" Pittsburgh said.

The man laughed. "That my twin brother Wang. He one of her dancers. My name Dong."

"Identical twins?"

"Twins. Yes!"

"Well, glad to meet you, Dong. I'm Pittsburgh, in charge of décor and set dressing."

~⊙

The crowd had dispersed and Sheriff Clement Jones—"Clem" to his deputies Hank and Jake—was glad to call it a night. Now all that was left to do was truck the sawhorses over to J.O. North Square to be used as barricades to separate the crowd from the news media in the morning. Clem was a six-foot, 175 lean-and-mean pounder, with a square jaw and a face like the surrounding countryside. Women, at least most women—which did not include his wife who had run off with an ex-con—found the craggy cheeks and jaw bones attractive.

The sheriff and Hank—he had dismissed Jake for the night—loaded the sawhorses into the back of the pickup. Clem was glad April East had arrived and was now settled in, and the media had gone off to Lil's, the local saloon. It had been one hell of a two weeks and he was tired. Tomorrow would not be better but at least it would be the last day. There hadn't been so much fuss in Timbuckone as far back as he could remember.

"I bet you'll be glad to git home to your wife."

"Yup," Hank answered.

Clem was looking up at the lights on the seventh floor of the hotel. "Wonder what people see in her?"

"Sex," Hank said.

"Funny," Clem chuckled as they drove toward the Square, "for some reason she don't turn me on."

"Well, maybe you're a hard man to turn on. Most ain't." And then wondering if maybe—in light of recent events and speculation about Clem's wife—he'd overstepped his bounds, Hank said, "If the opportunity arose, I sure as hell wouldn't kick her out of bed!"

As the courthouse clock struck midnight, Pittsburgh stood for a moment looking up at the hotel's facade. The Greek Revival with its falcon-gargoyle rain spouts had a Gothic look, he thought, as eddies of filmy dark clouds swirled in opposite directions against the moon. From the distance came the howl of a prairie wolf.

Pittsburgh shuddered as if feeling a sudden chill.

Chapter VI

"**G**ood morning, America."
From her place on the Early American green vinyl sofa in the rec room in Sandusky, Eunice said, "Sounds like he's afraid he's gonna wake someone up."

Joe attempted to ignore the sarcasm.

The TV camera had been panning the area just outside the Bijou Theatre and J.O. North Square, which was crowded with satellite and microwave vans. Television crews were scurrying around and it was only moments before African-American Anchorman Mickie Dunley and his blonde co-anchor, May Vap, took their places on the air, live.

"Here we are in Timbuckone, North Dakota."

The image was of flat country behind which a gigantic sun rose. A jack rabbit skipped lightly across the open space and disappeared into the shadow of a grain elevator. Then the image dissolved, revealing rugged terrain.

"That's not central North Dakota," Eunice said. "That's the badlands of South Dakota."

". . . Gullies so deep that early settlers avoided the area as impenetrable. Yet we are in the very heart of the heartlands, the geographical center of North America."

"Bullshit!" Eunice said. "They must have a second unit crew further south because the area where East was born is flat as a pancake."

The sound of *America the Beautiful* came in under the image of a pheasant wandering across the open space.

"See there? Flat as a pancake!"

"Flat, yeah. You should know something about that," Joe said.

"We are here because that great Hollywood legend, April East, is making a MTV video for the Hollywood Disaster Relief Fund and this is where she got her start."

An image on the set of a square dwelling on the prairie.

"That's one of those sod-walled huts," Eunice said.

"Humble beginnings? Perhaps. But to those of the old country, 'masses yearning to breathe free.'"

An image of a mean-looking couple holding shotguns.

". . . it was a land of opportunity where by dint of pluck, grit and sweat-equity their dreams could come true. And so it came to pass."

"That looks like Calamity Jane and her outlaw buddy, Wild Bill."

"When their daughter was only thirteen she caught the eye of lumber baron, J.O. North," May Vap said.

An image of a wedding picture showing a robust man in his late sixties standing over a décolleté April.

"If she'd been born a cow she'd have made some dairy farmer a fortune," Eunice chuckled.

"Shut up!" Joe snapped.

"Shortly after the marriage, a road company, headed by that great Italian actor, Luigi Stallone . . ."

An image of Stallone in tights enacting a Shakespearian role.

Eunice scoffed, "That's one of them codpieces."

". . . was stranded near Bismarck by a snowstorm and thereby a chance encounter . . ."

"Chance, my Aunt Fanny!"

"Quiet!"

"The actor immediately recognized her talents."

"Yeah, I'll bet! Both of 'em."

"And persuaded her husband to allow her to join his company."

"What a jerk *he* must have been," Eunice commented.

"Courageously, the young bride left Timbuckone and the following year was starring on The Great White Way."

An image of Broadway filled the screen.

"In M. Winterset Toms's smash hit, *Tura-Lura, Lay*."

Eyes downcast, April is pictured in a tightly wrapped Polynesian sarong being converted by Reverend Kavison to Christianity.

"But back in Timbuckone, J.O. North, lonely for his child bride and anxious for her return, built . . ."

Picture in sepia of the newly constructed Bijou Theatre.

". . . an exact replica of New York's finest theatre and hired theatrical impresario, Avid Plasco, to plan a season of classical revivals providing Timbuckone with culture, and his young wife with a series of leading men— including the famed Italian actor Guido Nadzo—to play with."

"Yeah, I'll bet!"

"It was here that she cut her teeth on the Bard's immortal *Romeo and Juliet*."

April leans over an ornate balcony toward Romeo.

"If those things had popped out, it might have been Notso Goodo for Guido Nadzo!"

"Pipe down, goddamn it!" Joe yelled.

"The production was quickly followed by Machiavelli's masterpiece, *Man Drag, O-Lay!*"

Imaged in a low cut Renaissance gown, April accepts the Holy Eucharist as she kneels at the altar of Saint Peter's Basilica backed by altar boys and Vatican soldiers.

"Those Swiss Guards are butted up real close to those choirboys."

"Will you stop it!" Joe bellowed.

"It was during this production that her beloved husband, J.O. North, died from a seizure of apoplexy."

"I shouldn't wonder."

April is at the funeral being supported by Stallone.

"Wow! Look at the low-cut on those widow's weeds."

"If you don't shut up . . ."

"Thus, tragically widowed and overcome with grief, she sought succor in Hollywood . . ."

"I'll bet!"

". . . where she made her meteoric rise. First in the classic role of the Holy Mother Mary . . ." April kneels below the cross, backed by muscular centurions. ". . . quickly followed by *Lady With A Lamp* as nurse Florence Nightingale." April leans over a soldier wounded during the Crimean War.

"Look at those bug eyes on that wounded soldier!"

"I'm tellin' ya for the last time to shut the hell up!" Joe yelled.

"And then she went modern with a light comedy, *A Chicken In Every Pot.*" April drops a chicken in a large pot. "President Hoover credited her with upping the out-of-work-American male's morale in a time of economic crisis. For this he awarded her the coveted Medal of Freedom." At the White House ceremony Hoover pins the Medal on April East's chest.

"And does Hungry Herb's wife look pissed, or what?" Eunice chortled.

Joe turned, swung and missed.

As soon as she realized what had happened, Eunice got up from the green vinyl couch and stormed upstairs to their bedroom. Turning profile, she looked in the mirror at the flatness of her chest. Then, with the aid of the bedpost, she got down on her knees and reached under the bed.

Back in the rec room, she carefully sighted along the gun's barrel as her index finger found the trigger's cold steel. The sound was deafening and the thirty inches of screen that was picturing April in a transparent low-cut gown in Las Vegas shattered into a million pieces.

Joe turned slowly to see his wife of fifty-eight years lower the shotgun.

༺⁃༻

Before Mickie Dunley could read his next line, there came the howl of a prairie wolf. Both Mickie and May turned instinctively in the direction of the wail, which came from the countryside on the other side of J.O. Square, now cluttered with the paraphernalia of the communication super highway.

And although she hated his guts, May Vap drew closer to Mickie in the sudden silence that filled the air space of *Good Morning America*.

Chapter VII

A single pilot light spread its glow into the stark reality of the shadowy backstage. The set, a replica of April East's Hollywood salon, was a nightmare of white, gold, and mirrors with an ivory baby grand piano on which rested an oriental bowl on a fringed serape; a large gold leaf frame held a photograph of East, next to a sepia miniature of her parents, and an alabaster nude statue, full Rubinesque, buttocks facing the audience. Stage-right was a Louis Seize sofa covered in a white and gold striped brocade, balanced by matching wing chairs of the same material.

Upstage, in the back wall, was a Gothic window seat framed by moss green velvet curtains through which could be seen Tinsel-town's Hills and the famous whitewashed spelling out of HOLLYWOOD. The set was mounted on a slightly raked parquet-floored platform, in front of which, stage level, were two canvas directors' chairs. On the canvas strip backing of one was spelled NICOLA SABBATINI and the other, APRIL EAST. Surrounding the set were standing "trees" (vertical iron pipes, plus a labyrinth of pipes overhead) on which hung more than a hundred lighting instruments. In the wings, four old stage hands, who hadn't hung a show in decades but were members of the father-son union, the local International Alliance of Theatrical Stage Employees, Moving Picture Technicians, Artists and Allied Crafts of the United States, Its Territories and Canada, played poker.

"What's the game?"

"Five card draw."

At the prop table, Pittsburgh picked up the box of flowers just delivered by FedEx. Moving on stage, he hummed/sang, "Pull yourself up/ Brush yourself off/ And begin once again/ Begin once again, begin once again/Till you've reached the end/Then do it again."

A demo of the CD had been sent to all crew heads for pre-production planning. Of course he recognized these lyrics as a rip-off of the Astaire and Rogers 1936 film *Swing Time.* It was a long song about various disasters throughout the country's history and always ended with these lyrics which put a positive spin on the country's endurance, ability and survival. But this tune was caught in his head and he could not rid himself of it.

Sliding his hand beneath the box to see if any moisture had leaked through and determining that it had not, he placed the box on the piano bench and removed the lid. He was about to arrange them in the Ming vase when the sight of a hollow indent in one of the pillows on the Louis Seize sofa caught his attention. A stagehand must have been napping sometime during the night. How unprofessional! Placing the flowers back in the box, he vigorously plumped the offending pillow until it was restored to its original fullness. Replacing it, he heard the auditorium door open. The FedEx man must not have closed it properly. Squinting to see through the darkened house, he called out, "Who is it?"

"It's me, Luv."

"Mona!"

As she made her way down the aisle, she said breathlessly, "It was damn difficult getting away from his nibs."

"You're talking about the kid?"

"Well, not exactly a kid, believe me."

"Who is he?"

"Part of her retinue. I'm contracted to 'attend and keep him out of harm's way.' My God! What a night! I'm frazzled! He can't keep his hands away from . . . it's disguising! Most guys have a picture of their girlfriend in their wallets? He's got one of his fist! And trust me, he's no 'kid.' Lord! Human endurance has its limits."

"Where is he now?"

"Sleeping in, thank God! He was up all hours last night and the same on the train the night before."

"How perfectly awful for you. And you must have been looking forward to this gig as much as I was. 'But no one ever said it was gonna be easy/No one ever said/It wouldn't be hard' That's from the song."

"Catchy!" Mona, said going to the grand piano. "Let me hear it again."

As Pittsburgh sang the song again she quickly picked up the tune.

"Do it again," she said, this time playing full volume as he sang.

"I'd forgotten what a terrific singer you are!"

"Thanks," he said, "but we really shouldn't be using the piano at all."

"Why?"

"It's an unwritten law." Then, quoting, "Props should never be used except in rehearsals or performances."

"Well I just came over do a couple of quick things but mainly to touch base with you before the taping, but I can only stay a minute or so; I can't risk his waking up and me not there. That witch, Beulah, would throw a fit. So first—and we gotta make this fast—where were you when it struck?"

"I was there!"

"In Hollywood?"

"Exactly! Look at this." He pulled up his trouser leg and showed her the scar.

"Gracious! How'd you get that?"

"Crawling over razor wire!" He took a sudden memory-of-emotion moment to pull himself together before continuing. "I saw Hollywood just vanish, sink into the sea. It's hard to talk about."

Sensing his distress, she said, "Well, thank God the two of you got out in time!"

Being coupled in the same breath, as it were, with the legendary star brought tears to his eyes.

Mona comforted him with a hug. "How long you been out here in the boonies?"

"A week," Pittsburgh said. "So what are you going to be doing? She never allows anyone in her dressing room except Beulah, isn't that right?"

"Absolutely! And my main job is to take care of the kid. I'll just take it moment to moment and make it through each day and as soon as this taping is over we'll get together and toss off a couple."

"Deal! But when I saw her yesterday . . . what a thrill! You gotta admit she's still as gorgeous as ever," Pittsburgh said.

"Yankee Doodle Dandy! Born on the fourth of July! Can you believe? At her age?" She removed a thermometer from her pocket. "One of my duties is to check the backstage temperature." She shook it down and attempted to read it. "I could use a bit of light, Luv; it has got to be exactly . . ."

"I know, sixty-eight degrees," Pittsburgh cut in. Just like Hepburn. Cupping his hand he called up into the flies, "Hey, Sparks, throw some light on the situation, will ya?"

On a catwalk forty feet above the stage, an old man put down his yellowed copy of *The Police Gazette*. At the ancient light board he pulled up a rheostat disk, which brought up the overhead strips, sending light filtering down through the labyrinth of pipes and instruments, adding softness to the harshness of the illumination provided by the ghost light.

"What you think of our set?" Pittsburgh asked.

Mona took a moment. "Lovely! Absolutely lovely!"

"Did you notice the alabaster statue on the piano?"

"She'll love it!"

"Getting a replica of the Gladys Lewis Bush original in North Dakota was *not* easy."

"Well, as the song says, 'No one ever said . . .'"

Pittsburgh sang, "It was gonna be easy/No one said/ It wouldn't be hard . . ."

Pittsburgh gathered the flowers in his arms and followed her around while she checked the temperature in various parts of the backstage. "And what about these? Getting orange blossoms was no piece of cake, either."

"Her favorite flower! How'd you ever manage, Luv?"

"A couple of years ago, when I was on *The Indira Gandhi Story*, I met this Air India pilot—a Sikh—you know, with all the hair? He flew them in from Madras and FedEx delivered them early this morning."

"Incidentally, before I go, I might as well . . ." Mona moved toward the April East canvas director's chair.

"Watch that trapped section!"

"Where, Luv?"

"Right where you're about to step," Pittsburgh pointed. "It's an old trap lid, probably safe but you never know. We can't cover it because the historic preservationists are on our ass about not altering any structural details of the building."

Mona stepped around the trapped area and sat in the April East chair, moving from side to side.

"What are you doing?"

"Testing her chair to see that it's 'sturdy.' Just one of the duties outlined in the job description."

⁓↻

Two chartered buses carrying members of New York's Philharmonic Orchestra pulled up in front of the Bijou. Weary musicians de-boarded, yawning and stretching. It had been a long morning; an early flight from LaGuardia Airport to O'Hare and then a puddle jumper to Bismarck, followed by the bus ride up to Timbuckone. But as Conductor Shephard Thomas knew, the trip was absolutely necessary. The Arts and Humanities endowment had been cut to zero, and the orchestra—as with most arts organizations—was hovering on the brink of extinction. So when East demanded that Harry Jukes get the good-looking conductor to wield his baton for her comeback, Milkin/Bush promised to *donate* a cool tax-deductible million to the orchestra and pay all expenses for the gig.

～⌒

"Well, dear that's it," Mona said, "The temperature is just below seventy all over the stage. Now I gotta run." She started back up the aisle but stopped, turned, and looked once again at the set. "It's so weird. I've seen this room before."

"It was pictured in Life Magazine."

"That's it! Her salon in Hollywood. Ravenworld!"

"No, dear! It's not Ravenworld, not like the big black glossy bird. It's *Rav*-en, *Rav*enworld." He bared his teeth and snarled. "Ravenously, to feed greedily, devour, *Rav*enworld!"

A shaft of sunlight suddenly cut across the floor as the stage door opened and closed. "Don't let any air in here!" Mona called.

No one saw the figure in black enter the theatre, go up the rickety stairs to the mezzanine, and enter the screened-off stage box where it moved close to the edge to observe, unobserved.

A rumpled and early-morning J.O. entered. "Where have you been!" he howled at Mona, stamping a foot. At any time of day or night J.O. was bad news, but mornings seemed to bring out a particular malevolence in him. It occurred to Mona that maybe he was a deranged distant relative, much like the maiden aunt who lived in her parents' attic in Melbourne. All she was sure of was that he was her responsibility and as he sidled across the stage, a bottl'd spider, a foul hunch-backed toad, she was quick to change her tone of voice. "Good morning, Luv. Sorry to yell at you but I thought you were a backstage intruder."

"No," J.O. said, his voice the whine of a defective chain saw, "I'm not an intruder!"

Talk about a situation gone wrong! To put a positive spin on it, Mona indicated Pittsburgh.

"Let me present our set-dresser, Mr. O'Casey, Pittsburgh O'Casey."

"You said it the wrong way," J.O. snapped. "*I* should be presented to *him*."

Thinking back to the time the Queen had visited Melbourne and Australians had to learn presentation etiquette, she said quickly, "Pittsburgh, may I present Mr. J.O, a member of Miss East's party."

Not being exactly certain of the proper response, Pittsburgh gave a gracious little dip in J.O.'s direction.

Ignoring it, J.O. addressed Mona. "Have you checked her chair yet?"

"Oh, yes, I just did that, Luv."

J.O. sidled his way across the stage, looked at the chair for a moment, then sat in it and moved around violently. Resting back, he surveyed the stage and drew a crooked finger under his shirt collar. "It's warm in here."

"It's exactly sixty-eight degrees." Mona tried vainly to keep her annoyance from showing.

"Seems warmer," J.O. said, his attention now drawn to the fringed serape under the Ming vase on the piano. "That's much too new."

"The serape?" Pittsburgh asked.

"Yes."

"It's aged fringe!"

"It *looks* new."

"It's six hundred year old Basque Country fringe—from Spain!"

"The fringe on the piano in her Hollywood apartment was old. That *looks* new!"

A thin lipped Pittsburgh whipped out a single-edged razor blade from within the sewing apron strapped around his waist. "I'll distress it a little."

"She always likes things *exact*."

"So do I!" Pittsburgh said, vehemently attacking the fringe.

J.O. crossed downstage to the left proscenium arch and ran his hand along it. "Dust!"

"There's not a speck of dust in this entire theatre," Pittsburgh cried out. "I even dusted the flies!"

"What do you call that?" J.O. said, holding up his gloved right hand.

"Overworked!"

"What did you say?" J.O. snapped.

There was no point in locking horns with the little bastard. "Someone may have overlooked a speck. I'll get the feather duster from the prop table."

Just then the door off the lobby opened and a figure approached down the central aisle. "Hi, I'm Rimsky Horowitz, the accompanist."

Pittsburgh came forward, "Glad to meet you. I'm Pittsburgh O'Casey, the set dresser, Mr. Horowitz."

"Please, call me Rimmy."

"And this is Mona, Miss East's dresser and you might say general factotum."

"Hey, glad to meet you, Mona."

"Same here. I've always loved your work."

"How did you come by the name Pittsburgh?" Rimmy asked.

"My father was a big shot there; Irish Catholic and . . . then *me!*" Pittsburgh threw up his hands.

Malevolently curious, J.O. sidled in.

Rimmy looked down. "Well, and who have we here?"

"This is Mr. J.O.," Mona said.

Rimmy bent down and held out his hand, "Good morning, Little One."

"You're not Lennie Bernstein!" J.O. shot back.

"Well, no."

"Only Lennie was allowed to call me 'Little One.'"

"Sorry," Rimmy said.

"You may call me Mr. J.O!" Mischief done, the little one moved to the side of the stage where he sat on the steps leading to the auditorium, and wetting the lead in the pencil stub on his reddish cracked tongue he began laboriously writing in a spiral notebook.

Up in the stage box, the figure in black, having observed everything, exited the box. In the darkened corridor, the gnarled arthritic fingers emerged from the covering cloak and started punching in a text message on a Blackberry.

⌒〜〇

"Mornin'," the dance captain called out as he came through the stage door, followed by his dancers.

"Mona, Pittsburgh," Rimmy called, "Meet Peter, our dance captain, and the other dancers: Dick, Wang, and Putz."

"Hello, Luvs," Mona called.

In the deepest tone he could muster, Pittsburgh said, "Hi, guys."

Jack, the stage manager arrived and was introduced. The dancers began to stretch out in their warm-up outfits, which they progressively shed to reveal red, white and blue briefs, duplicates of the actual costumes they would wear for the taping.

It was time for the rehearsal to commence. Jack pressed the switch that automatically tracked the parquet floor platform down stage. As it was moving, Pittsburgh inspected the flowers in the Ming vase and moved upstage to check the window seat and drapes, while Rimmy organized his sheet music.

With everything ready, Peter called, "OK, we've rehearsed in New York for three weeks and we've got it down pat. So all we're doing now is getting used to being on stage and using the set. Let me say it once again. For the most part we're out here in front where the stage floor is flat. But I've blocked it so we do use the platform occasionally. As you can see it's raked slightly which means a slight adjustment in balance. And, now we've got the real set props which incidentally," he turned to Pittsburgh, "look absolutely terrific!" Clapping his hands, the others joined in. With a last minute plump to the pillows on the sofa, Pittsburgh blushed with pleasure.

"So let's go through those sections where we shift from the stage floor to the raked platform. Rimmy, give us the eight beats before her entrance." Peter counted, "Uh, five, six, seven, eight . . ."

～⌒๑

Inside the portable dressing room on stage left, April put down the Blackberry and turned to Beulah who was reading the *New Amsterdam News*. "I thought you were supposed to see that the little bastard stayed out of sight."

"That Mona's job!"

"We know we can't count on her; she's not one of us. Now go out there and see where he is."

In a bitter exaggerated dialect, accompanied by a little soft-shoe-Stepin-Fetchit-shuffle, Beulah said, "Yes'm, Miz East, I'll sure find 'im for you."

～⌒๑

Pittsburgh saw Beulah exit the dressing room and waddle toward the stage. All he could see was Aunt Jemima on the pancake box. It was hard for him to believe that the outfit she wore was Miss East's choice. She liked to dress herself the same as she did at the height of her fame, but would she have insisted on keeping Beulah in that awful Mammy outfit?

In his heart, Pittsburgh knew, that for all her risqué banter, Miss East was really a good person. He remembered the stories about how devastated she was when Beulah the First died that horrible death from a rattlesnake bite while she picnicked in the desert. Miss East had buried her—as if she were a relative—at Forest Lawn and installed carillons in her mausoleum that perpetually played Al Jolson singing *My Mammy*.

Seeing Beulah coming, J.O. quickly put the spiral notebook in his shirt pocket and started up the aisle in a hasty retreat.

"Boy! You stop right der in yo' tracks!" Beulah commanded.

Terrified, J.O. did as he was told.

"Mistuh J.O., Miz East been wonderin' where you was."

"Why now?" J.O. said under his breath.

"You suppose to be wid Miss Mona!"

"I just been out here." J.O. indicated the auditorium.

"What you been doin' out here, boy?" Beulah asked in an unmistakably sinister quality, as though she already knew the answer.

"Just . . . checking," J.O. said.

"Checkin' what?"

J.O. did not respond.

"What you been checkin', boy?" Beulah asked, giving a quick look at the dancers. Then waddling down the steps, she said in a low voice, "You ain't been writin' none of that nastiness again, has you?"

"Oh, no!" J.O. said in mock surprise. "Honest."

Beulah held out her hand. "Let me see, boy!"

J.O.'s eyes darted as though obeying confused brain signals. For the first time in memory he had been on his own without supervision and the taste of freedom was sweet. Turning suddenly, he ran up the aisle toward the door to the lobby. Beulah's voice was a powerful baritone command. "Boy! You stop right der in yo' tracks!"

Rimsky stopped playing, the dancers stopped dancing, and the technicians, who had joined the company within the last half hour, stopped working.

Above in the stage box, the figure in black had returned to observe.

Beulah took her time moving up the aisle. "You bin writin' some of that nastiness against your mommy dearest, ain't you?" She jabbed her index finger against J.O.'s caved in chest. "Answer me, boy!"

J.O. was now reduced from a wizened old man to a puling child. Twisting his shirt tail with his fingers, he smiled slyly up at the big black woman. "Honest, Beulah . . ."

"All this writin' comes from watchin' those *Sesame Street* re-runs," Beulah said menacingly. "Writin' nasty *slander* which you hope to get published against our dearest Miz East."

"I am not!"

Grabbing J.O.'s spindly arm and holding him immobile, Beulah thrust her other hand into his right pants pocket. J.O. immediately started giggling and the sound changed to hysterical shrieks as he fell onto the aisle's red carpet. Beulah reached into his shirt pocket and withdrew the spiral notebook with the pitiful stub of pencil tucked inside the coiled spirals. "I thought so!" she said triumphantly, and opened the notebook and read the infantile handwriting. "I wanted to sit next to Guido but the mean bitch made me sit in the box with Beulah so no one would know."

"You know what our dearest Miz East always say?" Beulah asked, looking down at the convulsing body.

"Ye . . . ye . . . yes!" he gasped, asthmatically.

Beulah pulled him to his feet and shook him. "Then you say it, boy! Say it!"

Terrified, J.O. started to recite, "How. . . How. . . How sharper . . ."

"That's it, boy! Go on!" Beulah shook him again. "How sharper . . ."

". . . than a serpent's tooth it is, to have a . . ."

"Say it!"

". . .thankless child," J.O. said, breaking into sobs.

Releasing him, Beulah raised her big hands toward the heavens and shouted, "Hallelujah! Praise de Lord! Dat's de troof! He born again!" And then looking back at the boy, added, "Who said 'How sharper than a serpent's tooth'? Who say dat?"

"God," J.O. said through his sobs.

"Praise His name!" Beulah said. She ripped the offensive pages from the notebook, tore them into several pieces, and swallowed them. Handing the notebook back, she leaned over and whispered menacingly into his ear, "Don't ever let me catch you writin' impudence 'gainst your Mama Dearest ever again, you hear? You know she got a weak heart."

"Yes, Ma'am," J.O. whispered.

Beulah turned to the stage where the company stood gaping. "Well, what you lookin' at?" she demanded. "Git back to work!"

Rimsky started to play. The dancers resumed dancing and the technicians hurried back to various tasks so that once again the sound of rehearsal filled the theatre and took away the awful silence.

Beulah waddled on stage. "I thought we agreed that you're supposed to look after him," she said to Mona.

"Sorry."

"Is the temperature right in here?"

"As right as it can be," Mona replied.

"What do that mean?" Beulah asked.

"Sixty-eight degrees."

"Why don' you say so in da first place?"

As Beulah sat in April East's special chair, moving her weight back and forth, checking the pins securing it, she thought that perhaps it wasn't a bad idea to let J.O. run amuck—something drastic was needed to rid the entourage of him—and given enough rope maybe she could hang him. She was thinking this as she squatted beside the chair and found its holding pin. Then rising and slapping her hands to the music, she lifted her skirt to reveal a red petticoat. "Mr. Rhett, he give it to me," she explained to no one in particular as she danced along the stage, and sang,

"Pull yourself up/ Brush yourself off/ And begin once again/ Begin once again, begin once again/Till you've reached the end/ Then do it again."

J.O. watched her, his small eyes filled with hate.

Chapter VIII

M ost of the crew, except for Pittsburgh, had worked straight through till two a. m.—which meant overtime—but had to miss the entrance of their star into the Hotel Bismarck, a real disappointment. There was the usual winding down, drinking and getting to bed about four and back to the theatre at ten where there was, as there *always* was, the heaping tables of food: bagels, coffee, tea, lox and cream cheese, jams, jellies, quiche, scrambled eggs, bacon, sausage, muffins, toast, orange juice, grapes, and dry cereal. Following the culinary camaraderie was a half-hour call.

The Bijou erupted into the sounds of final preparation: a cacophony of instruments tuning up in the orchestra pit along with the noise made by a swarm of young, highly-trained full-of-themselves technicians shouting orders on stage, in the wings, the flies, the cat-walks, the auditorium, re-gelling lights, checking boom microphones, spots, chasers, flashing lasers, and moving shafts of back light. It was an army of guys.

Pittsburgh had to acknowledge that April East was not an equal opportunity employer. All worked decisively but respectfully around the old IATSE poker players. The electricians had strung miles of cable taped with silver tape to floors and walls of the old theatre. Platforms with dollies had been rigged to transport cameras over auditorium seats and onto the stage. An air of total confusion— organized chaos—reigned.

Fifteen minutes prior to the scheduled rehearsal, Nick Sabbatini appeared with his interpreter. He wore a black Giorgio Armani suit, light blue shirt unbuttoned halfway to his navel revealing a gold chain on which hung a silver cross nestled in a thicket of curly black chest hairs. To maintain the illusion of an Italian film director, Suzie and he had decided that he speak only in Italian, which she would translate.

Making his way onto the stage, he stood for a moment in solitary reverie, looking out at the old ornate auditorium. Then turning and facing the platform where Pittsburgh was bent over dusting beneath the piano, Nick cried out, "Bello. Bellissimo! Bravo, Signor Williams. Anzi, bravissimo!"

A startled Pittsburgh, rising too quickly, bumped his head and whispered to one of the dancers, "Is he talking to me?"

Suzie explained. "No. He is complementing the design."

He was disappointed but was used to having the set designer get all the credit. No one ever recognized the set dresser's creative contribution, Pittsburgh thought.

"I'll tell Stewie when I see him,"

"Hollywood, Hollywood! Perduto!" Nick said with great emotion.

Beulah scowled. "What's he carryin' on about?"

"Mr. Sabbatini laments the loss of Hollywood," Suzie answered.

Nick addressed Peter, "Sono pronti i ballerini per la Signorina East?"

"Are the dancers ready to rehearse the beginning for Miss East?" Suzie interpreted.

"Yes, we can do the whole number if she wants to see it," Peter answered.

"Mr. Sabbatini understands that Miss East wishes only to see the first part. She is superstitious about doing a complete run-through before the actual take. She just wants to check out the dancers."

Standing nearby, dancer Putz understood exactly what was implied. It had been rumored that in the old days, East used male dancers not only for their ability in the art of Terpsichore but for their athleticism in the sack.

"You hear that?" He nudged Wang.

"Hot dog!" Wang said. "She's been eye-balling me in rehearsals."

"Attenzione! Per piacere!"

"Attention, please!" Suzie called.

A score of assistant directors throughout the theatre called for quiet, although by this time they were the only ones making any noise.

"Signore e signori. Compagni. Amici," Nick said.

"Company. Friends."

"Operatori."

"Cameramen." Suzie signed as she spoke.

"What's that for?" Beulah whispered to Mona.

"Anyone on the crew who is hearing challenged."

Beulah shook her head. "Deaf *and* dumb?"

"Elettricisti. Musicisti. Assistenti. La compagnia."

"Mr. Sabbatini greets you all."

While Nick was talking, Beulah shuffled off-stage to the portable dressing room and knocked.

"Who is it?"

"Me."

"Come in."

Beulah entered, leaving the door slightly ajar.

"Did you find the little bastard?" April asked.

"Yeah."

"Is he out of the way?"

"I'd like to see him out of the way for good!" Beulah said.

"Yeah, I know what you mean. He drives me nuts, too." She rotated her head to relax her neck muscles.

"You're strung way out," Beulah said.

"Yeah."

"You know what you need?"

"I could use a drink or a couple of tokes off of some good Colombian."

"Booze and drugs would only fuck up the performance but . . . I think maybe you could get a little action before this afternoon's taping."

"What'd you have in mind?"

"I saw you checking out that hayseed's package back in Bismarck. You need a little *re*laxation."

April took a moment before answering. "Yeah."

"That slant dancer?"

"Wang?"

"He's hot for you."

"You think so?"

"You know he's horny."

April brushed the powder puff against her cheek. It was true, she was as tight as Kelsey's balls. She could feel the tension in her shoulders, neck and stomach. It had been years since she appeared before an audience. At the beginning, she took private classes and had a trainer to keep her in shape. But as weeks turned into months and months into years the daily routine became perfunctory. And then the tsunami and Madam's idea for the video. And in the last four weeks she had been on pills, a killer diet, exercise, and rehearsals and now as the event approached . . . well, damn right she was stressed!

Beulah drew close to the make-up table and whispered, "It's been a long time . . ."

"Yeah," April said.

It *had* been a long time and she *had* checked Wang out during rehearsals. He was kinda cute. She was tempted, had been tempted all the way across the country by the various hunks in the photo ops. But it was the hayseed at Bismarck—his sudden shyness—that brought her desire back into full focus. It would have been so easy, she could have had him . . . but she'd been warned.

"È una giornata storica per due motivi: il ritorno di April East..."

She heard the workers' applause at the mention of her name. It had been an awful long time for that as well. She moved to the dressing room door to listen. Then on impulse and still in her kimono, she stepped out on to the stage and undulated her way toward the light.

None of the crew facing Nick onstage saw her until she gave out with a husky, "Excuse me, boys." When one of the men recognized her, she held her finger to her lips for silence.

The man, Phil Kelly, was dumbstruck. He had worked on her last film many years ago and he would swear she looked exactly the same. The others, younger men who had only seen her in the caricatures drawn by Norse of Norway and in screenings in their film history classes at USC and SUNY Purchase grew silent, respectful.

Respect was not what she wanted. These kids were a new breed. April East was used to the give-and-take of the old time crewmen when guys were guys and dames, dames. She'd have to warm the youngsters up.

"Abbiamo deciso di aiutare la California," Nick was saying.

"And to give disaster relief to the victims," Suzie interpreted.

"Sará un atto d'amore per le famiglie."

"He says that our work today will be an act of love dedicated to the families of those who perished."

". . . Malgrado tutti i disastri, America deve sempre essere l'America, un paese forte che sa rinascere. Per citare il vostro illustre presidente, 'L'America sopravvive e va avanti!'"

". . . that despite this terrible disaster, despite *all* the terrible disasters mentioned in her song, as our President so eloquently said, 'America survives and advances!'"

Moving through the clusters of crewmen, creating ripples of silence, April came to the wings, paused a moment and taking a deep breath to slow her pounding heart, walked out on stage. As the rest of the crewmen saw her, she held up her hand for silence while Nick, who was facing the auditorium, finished and waited for the applause that never came.

Hands on slow gyrating hips, April watched the panicked Nick, who looked toward Suzie for help and found her gazing speechless across the stage. Turning, he was stunned to see her.

Now was the time to take over, the way East had always taken over. To show the company who was in charge. "Excuse me, Mr. Director," she said, "who does a girl have to fuck around here to get a little ah-tense-z-own-ee?"

One of the IATSE card players, who had left the game and come on stage, wheezed, "Miz East! By God, you lookin' good enough to eat!"

"Thanks, Baby," she said, moving stage center. "Did we ever *know* each other in the old days?"

And the way she said it—wiggling her ass—made each of the crewmen remember the Norse of Norway pictures: the large succulent breasts, rounded thighs, full muscular buttocks, and split-beaver. And the stunned silence that greeted her entrance changed to boisterous laughter, applause and cheers, filled with raw sexual energy.

It was exactly what she needed.

In the booth the sound designer said, "Let's give her a real welcome." His assistant flipped the switch of the applause track, careful the enhancement would not override the actual sound of the men on stage.

The Living Legend absorbed the welcome, acknowledging the army of workers, loving their acclaim because she loved to be loved. The ovation lasted well over a minute before she silenced them. Peering into the auditorium, she called, "To all you great cameramen out there." And then noticing the elderly Chinese man she had been told about, "Especially my old favorite, James . . . One-Hung-Low." Holding for the laugh, she turned to the right wing and then to the left. "And to all you big easy stage hands," and looking up to the electric fly gallery, she called, "You too, Sparks, and all the 'sparks' in my life." The entire stage became brilliantly lit.

Undulating forward, knowing she had won over any skeptics, she leaned into the orchestra pit. "And Shephard, you gorgeous hunk and all your gorgeous catgut scrapers and horn blower virtuosos . . ."

The musicians sounded their instruments in response.

Then facing toward the balcony, April East spread her arms wide and cried, "I'm back, Boys!"

Sparks hit her with a special pink-gelled pin-point spot and halo back lighting. "How do I look?"

The response was deafening. At the peak of the ovation—his timing was impeccable—Pittsburgh stepped forward.

East frowned. There was a clause in her contract that no one unauthorized was to approach her within twenty feet and he was too damn close.

Beulah stepped forward and whispered, "He's representing the A.F. of L., the C.I.O. and the locals, numbers one through twelve, of the Set Dressers of America, plus their affiliates."

Since no one was going to do it, and Mona was the sole crew member of the female sex, she moved in and said, "He was chosen to greet you on behalf of the crew." And then for everyone to hear, she introduced him, "Pittsburgh O'Casey, our set dresser; Miss East."

Pittsburgh bowed.

"What you got on your mind?" April said, hands on undulating hips.

Although he had gone over the speech a hundred times, Pittsburgh was nervous. Lowering the pitch of his voice he said,

"On behalf of all of us and, and, and . . . speaking person . . . al . . . ly . . . I want to say, that this is . . . well, that working with you is the greatest honor of my life. And, and, I know I speak for all of us on the crew when I say, I shall cherish . . . this moment, always."

As soon as he said 'cherish' he began to lose it.

For all her brashness, April was suddenly moved to see this grown man, tears welling up in his eyes. "That's real sweet of you, baby, and I'm honored," she said, brushing a hand against his cheek. Then, lest the moment become serious, lest she complicate her own one-dimensional image, she was 'on' again, like a stand-up comic playing to a full Saturday night house. "Just tell the boys you represent, . . ." she placed her right hand at the décolletage of her costume " . . to keep on plumpin' them pillows!"

The bad boys went crazy.

Pittsburgh dipped, stepped back three paces and turned away. Nick now commanded the star's attention, and, as in a mating dance, she moved around him, scanning him up and down.

With malice and thinly disguised timidity, J.O, in humiliated exile in the darkened auditorium, heard the hosannas. Seeing the bitch's openly expressed sexual interest in the Italian director, he tiptoed up the steps to the stage. Right hand in his pants pocket fondling himself, a smirk on his face, he stared at the silver cross nestled in Nick's thick black chest hair.

April whispered to Beulah, "Get that little bastard out of here."

Grabbing J.O.'s arm, Beulah jerked his face into the oblivion of her breasts.

"Mamammmm . . ." came the smothered cries.

Carrying him to the auditorium and slamming him into a seat, Beulah hissed, "If you get up again, I'll break your fucking arm!"

Suzie, witnessing this humiliation of the . . . boy? man? . . . by the big black woman felt sorry for him and could not help but wonder if she had heard correctly. Did he say 'Mama'? She turned to Nick, but his attention was fixed on his star.

"OK, Mr. Director," April said, "why don't you show me what you got?"

"Signorina East, è un grande onore!"

Suzie moved forward. "He says it is a great honor."

"Non dimenticheró mai la Sua magnifica interpretazione nel ruolo della Maria Vergine!"

He says he will never forget your magnificent portrayal as Mother Mary.

Recovering from the hot flush he felt during his welcoming speech, Pittsburgh was thoroughly delighted at Nick's remembrance of Miss East's first major hit.

"Quando ha dato uno schiaffo a Basil Rathbone. Indimenticabile!"

". . . that unforgettable moment when you slapped Basil Rathbone," Suzie interpreted.

Pittsburgh flashed back to his film history class at Carnegie Tech. His hand shot up, waving for recognition. Not getting it, he cried out, "Excuse me. EXCUSE ME!"

There was sudden silence.

He moved to Nick. "It wasn't just the slap. She slapped his *right* cheek."

Everyone turned.

"Destra, sinistra, che importanza ha?"

"How is that important?" Suzie said gently, smiling.

Pittsburgh gasped. "No other actress could have done it!"

"Well, I don't exactly remember the *de*tails." East said, undulating.

Pittsburgh was very excited. "No other actress had the capability!"

"Fu un momento incredibile!" Nick said to Suzie at the same time April whispered to Beulah, "What the hell's this geek talkin' about?"

"You slapped his right cheek!" Pittsburgh said. "Don't you remember?"

"Left cheek, right cheek . . . what's the diff, Kid?" April said.

Pittsburgh was stunned. "It was the whole point," he said. "See," he demonstrated to Nick, "Miss East was holding out her left hand in supplication to Rathbone who was playing the evil Pontius Pilot . . . and because the shot was over his left shoulder, she had to slap his right cheek with the palm of her right hand. *Anyone* could have slapped the left cheek, but only Miss East could have slapped the right cheek with any grace! Don't you see? That was the reason for her extraordinary success! She was double jointed! And not only in her right elbow, her right wrist as well!"

"Certo. Ha ragione!"

"He says, 'of course you're right'," Suzie interpreted.

"Well, I always figured two joints were better than one!" April said, without missing a beat.

The crew broke into laughter.

"That's what I told my director, Mr. Da Mayo, when I played Saint Joan," April said, warming to the situation.

Pittsburgh moved in quickly. "No, No, *Made in Orleans* was not directed by Louis Da Mayo! Da Mayo directed *Lady with a Lamp!*"

Nick understood at once. "Ma certo! Non era Da Mayo. Fu De Koven il regista del film!"

Pittsburgh emphatically shook his head in agreement.

"Well . . ." April said to the crew, "yeah, it *was* De Koven. What the hell? Whoever remembers directors?"

There was great laughter.

"Now let's stop horsin' around and get this show on the road!" She sprang into action, turning to the dancers. "Hey, boys, whatya say we do a little work?"

"OK by us," Peter said.

"Maestro!" she called to Rimsky. "How about me doin' the intro and then I'll stand out and see what the guys have got." She called out to the older Chinese cameraman, "Jimmy, you can see what we're up to and get it this afternoon. You know me, Baby, I've always been a one-shot take."

There were cheers and applause.

Pittsburgh moved in. "Except for that final scene after Essex's execution in *Good Queen Bess*." Turning to Nick, he added as a point of information, "Damoulian was directing." Then back to April, "What do you want here? you asked." Then in a perfect imitation of Damoulian's Hungarian accent, as he had done with hers, he continued, "Nothing here. You don't act here. Just make your face a blank. Think of nothing, feel nothing, try not even to blink your eyes. Make your face a *tabula rasa,* a blank page on which the spectator will write his own ending."

East gave Beulah a 'get-rid-of-the-bastard' nod and said, "I remember it wasn't an easy scene to act."

"It took forty-seven takes!" Pittsburgh enthused, "but it is the greatest moment in the history of films!"

"Let's kill the remembrances, Tiger," April said. She started snapping her fingers, turned to Shephard Thomas in the pit, and said, "OK, Maestro, hit it!" Flinging off her kimono to reveal the red, white and blue tights, she was on the parquet stage in front of her dancers, singing.

༺༻

The subject of the CD was disasters endured by Americans. The point of each was how Americans accepted them with the indomitable spirit of survivalists, extolling each disaster with a positive spin. The first, on the Civil War, included references to the 620,000 deaths and casualties, the assassination of Lincoln and the reconstruction, with emphasis on the survival of the union. Five more disasters followed in the same razzmatazz show business mode all ending with East in a blaze of glory.

So what did we do?
Moan and cry?

Throw up their hands
And want to die?

Hell no! Cause . . .

No one ever said
Life would be easy
No one ever said
It wouldn't be hard

Soooooooooooooo
Pull yourself up
Brush yourself off
And begin once again
Begin once again,
Begin once again,
till you reach the end
Then do it again

Nick was entranced. The music, the dancers, April East singing with a rhythm, a control that was magnificently her own; there was no one like her. Never had been, never would be. Camp? Sure, she invited parody, and the song was a pastiche. Nothing in it was original; styles were superimposed on one another causing a sense of dislocation since nothing was connected. She sang with a cool disdain for the musical thefts, so that what transpired became entirely original. Goddamn it! She was *post* postmodern! And there was magic in it, transforming, beautiful, up-beat magic.

Sparks had started throwing in the special rock-show chaser, lasers and back lighting. And although this was only an impromptu run-through and he knew she was holding back so that the full effect would not be there until the actual performance, it was enough to forecast what would transpire that afternoon when she did the actual taping. It was going to be one hundred percent sexy eye-candy *commercial*, the best of Hollywood, Broadway, Las Vegas, Disney World, and MTV and *nobody* did that better than HOLLYWOOD, U. S. of A. No*body!*

As she sang, April felt the magic, and at the end of the first section she knew that she had her audience of technicians—the toughest audience in the world—spellbound. So she walked away, out of the light, toward the chair with her name on it, to observe the action on stage and to check out Wang, whom she was seeing for the first time in his dance belt costume.

Beulah smiled as East sat down. The chair collapsed with a dull thud; like a string-less puppet, the great Hollywood legend sprawled on her ass on the floor.

Chapter IX

Sheriff Clem Jones was back stage when the chair collapsed. He was there because a manager type working the show asked him to 'stand by,' and before he had time to think the thing through the guy had thrust two one-hundred dollar bills into his hand. He wondered if he should give it back. He was already being paid $28,000 a year as sheriff. Would this be some kind of conflict of interest? But then again—he was on call twenty-four hours a day so the money wasn't that good, one reason why his wife had left—and if anything *did* happen, Jake, his part-time assistant, could call him on his cell phone. If it wasn't for the two, one-hundred dollar bills now in his wallet he'd probably be with Jake on crowd control out in J.O. Square.

When April East sprawled out on the floor, everything didn't stop all at once. It was kind of a wind down. The four guys dancing froze, then the piano player, and the guys offstage who could see what had happened. But it was a while before the conductor stopped waving his baton and the musicians stopped playing.

Clem's attention was immediately drawn to the big black woman and the runt because of the expressions on their faces. Although they were not looking at each other directly, each was smiling a *mean* smile.

"Son of a bitch!" East yelled.

And then the hullabaloo started.

The funny acting guy they called the set dresser (Clem had come to think of him as 'the funny duck') was the first to reach her, kneeling and holding her hands. Then the runt ran up screaming, "MaMaMaMa!" and the chief honcho who spoke Italian said something to the pretty brunette gal—Clem had first noticed her when he came in the theatre and in truth she was the reason he stayed—and she called for ice water.

"Fuck the water, get me a drink," East yelled.

Clem wasn't exactly used to that kind of talk, especially from a woman, but he wasn't offended; actually it amused him.

The Funny Duck got up and pushed his way through the mob, the runt yelled "Mama," and Ms. East yelled, "Mona! Where the hell are you?" and then screamed at the runt, "Get away from me, you little shit!" The brunette asked if there was anything she could do and the star said in a syrupy voice, "Yeah! run out and get me a ham and cheese on rye and tell 'm to hold the mayo."

The brunette got up and started off, then stopped, turned, and Clem figured she got the idea. She'd been sent up. Show people were an odd lot.

The Italian said something and the brunette asked Ms. East if she was all right. "No," she answered, "I always do this for the warm up." Then the runt yelled "Mama!" again and East yelled, "Shut up!" The runt threw himself on the floor, screaming and kicking his legs and pounding his fists. East yelled and the Italian said something and the brunette said something to East about not straining her voice and she yelled back, "That's all anyone cares about." The runt's temper tantrum got worse and the star yelled to the black woman, "I told ya to shut that damn kid up!" Clem could see that the brunette didn't much cotton to the abuse the runt was getting. The tall white dancer moved East's legs, probably checking for broken bones. The Mexican-American dancer ran in with a pitcher of ice water, but The Funny Duck got there first with a pint bottle and a glass. East grabbed the bottle and chugged down a big swallow. Then another outburst from the runt and East yelled, "Can't anyone shut him up?" The black woman grabbed one of his flaying arms, yanked him to his feet, and slapped her palm over his mouth. The arm yanking was so fierce, Clem thought it might have been dislocated from the shoulder socket. Then the runt bit the black woman and she whammed him, shoving his face into her big bosom. Not a good move if the kid's a biter, Clem thought. The black woman lugged the muffled-voiced runt off the stage and Ms. East drank another slug of booze. That was the hullabaloo, and Clem wouldn't have believed it if he hadn't seen it with his own eyes and heard it with his own ears.

It was while Beulah was hauling the brat off that East noticed it—a momentary reflection of light that struck against steel— coming from one of the theatre boxes. She remembered suddenly: she was being watched, had been watched the whole time. And now she could be in trouble. Looking into the sea of faces surrounding her, she did what she thought would earn high marks.

"Clear off!"

Everyone moved except The Funny Duck, who helped her up. She slowly moved one leg and then the other, one arm and the other, then her neck and holding her head with her hands, twisted her jaw. Finally she shook herself all over, like a retriever just out of water. The Italian said something and the brunette asked, "He wants to know; are you all right?"

"He," she addressed the crew, pointing her thumb in Nick's direction, "wants to know if I'm 'all right.'" She laughed, tossing her head. "Hey, Pop!" she yelled to an older guy working crew, "Will April East go on with the show?"

"Fuckin-A!" he yelled back.

There were shouts of support.

"Will April East survive?" she bellowed.

"You're damn right!" the head electrician called, and this was followed by others throughout the theatre. "You know it, baby!"

"If you don't survive, ain't no one will."

"And is Hollywood gonna survive the Big One?" she howled.

"You better believe it!"

"We'll build again!"

Holding up her hand she cupped her ear. "I can't hear ya, boys!"

In the sound booth a technician flipped the switch for the sound track of the standing ovation given Sondheim's *Follies* at Avery Fisher Hall, a combination of applause, cheers, foot stamping, and whistles.

East held up her hand for silence. "That's better, guys!" she said, and turned to Shephard Thomas. "Maestro, take the second course."

A wave of relief swept over Pittsburgh as he realized she was playing the house, pumping up enthusiasm, readying them for the taping that afternoon. Thank God she had not gone deaf! Images of Jane Wyman as the mute in *Johnny Belinda* had played through his mind.

The workers returned to their places, Thomas raised his baton, Rimsky struck a note, the lasers and back lighting started, the dancers found their positions and April East, snapping her fingers, yelled, "So I fell on my ass so what do I do?"

> Blubber and whine?
> Tear out my hair
> Cry myself blind?
>
> Hell no! Cause . . .
>
> No one ever said
> It was gonna be easy
> No one ever said
> It wouldn't be hard

Soooooooooooooooo
I pull myself up
Brush myself off
And begin once again
Begin once again,
Begin once again
Till I've reached the end
Then…do it again!

Nick marveled. This time was as magical as the first but with an added incandescence, a feeling of everyone in the auditorium rooting for her, willing her on, lending their energy, wanting her to win, assuring her that she was still great, experiencing *through* her, the fall and the recovery which affirmed continuum, survival, greatness, and driving out the overwhelming knowledge that we all grow old and die.

Having watched all of it, the figure in black wheeled about and went from the stage box to the rickety elevator.

With surprising rapidity, the parquet floor tracked back, the lights were turned out, and the crew, along with the musicians, noisily departed the Bijou for their lunch break. Once again the stage was illuminated only by the single naked bulb from the ghost light.

The dancers had not been assigned separate dressing rooms. They were not modest about dressing and undressing. Wherever. As Peter told the stage manager who apologized for the lack of privacy, "Don't worry about it. There's not a man jack among us whose swinging dick can't be checked out on DVDs in the Adult section of your corner video store." Sweaty from rehearsal, they toweled down and got out of their costumes and into their sweats.

"Suppose she's gonna be OK?" Putz asked.

"Sure," Peter said. "Didn't she just prove it?"

"I heard she has a weak heart," Dick said.

Pittsburgh's reverie from her second chorus was broken by their chatter. On the pretext of tidying up, he went on the set and vigorously plumped one of the pillows on the sofa.

"She's tough. Takes more than a spill to kill that old broad."

"She may be old but she's still got that swing!" Wang said.

"Horny bastard." Peter pushed him aside. "That brother of yours . . . is he of the same persuasion?"

"No, Dong's gay."

"But other than that . . ."

"We're physically identical, except he's got a couple of inches on me."

"Identical twins and he's two inches taller?"

"Oh, no," Wang said. "We're the same height."

"Jeepers! These buns are uncomfortable," Putz said, removing the padding from the back of his briefs."

"They sure make your skinny ass look good, though," Peter said.

Pittsburgh was in shell shock. Maleness—bought in a package—now a cottage industry! He was not so much offended by the loose talk as he was by the cynicism of it. Was nothing sacred?

"You think it will be OK with wigs and hair if I just leave this on," Wang said pointing to his chest.

"I never understood why they wanted you to wear a chest toupee in the first place."

"She loves it. She said so in New York, and she incorporated that bit of running her hand through it."

"But Chinese men don't have chest hair."

"Well, this show ain't exactly in classic *Hamlet* 'holding-a-mirror-up-to-nature' style. This is showbiz and she gets what she wants. And you gotta admit she sure knocked everyone's socks off on that second chorus."

"Speaking of," Peter said, holding out his hand.

Wang reached inside his dance belt and tossed the rolled up sock to Peter.

"You can have it back for the taping."

"I sure hope she doesn't have any preconceptions about black dudes," Dick said nervously as he reached in his dance belt for the other sock. "That's been a hard myth to live down."

"I heard she gives great head," Putz said.

"I wouldn't mind a little head start," Wang said. "But I like the old-fashioned missionary position with its hydraulic action—the old in/out—with me on top!"

"Is that all those Baptists we sent to China taught you guys?" Dick asked.

"No hydraulic action with her. Head only. That's the story," Peter said.

Pittsburgh gasped. My God! As though April East would ever! He felt total indignation.

All conversation stopped suddenly as they watched Pittsburgh flounce off stage. "What do you suppose pulled his chain?" Peter asked.

Wang shook his head. "Pillow plumpers! Always on the rag."

It was at this moment that Beulah came hurrying on. "OK, Boys! Miz East done chose."

"Ch . . . chose?" Dick asked.

"That was a nasty fall she took." Beulah's tone was defensive. "She done need a little *re*laxation to take her mind off this afternoon's taping and to build up her confidence."

"*Re*laxation?" Dick asked.

"Don't worry, she ain't after one of da brothers." Turning to Wang, she said, "Miz East done chose you."

"Me?"

"I reckon she's hungry for a little Chinese!"

"*All right!*" Wang said, thumbs upping the others as he started off with his gym bag.

"Whoa, boy. Where you goin'?"

"Thought I'd take a quick wash-up." Wang held up an underarm and sniffed.

"Don't bother. She likes things a little gamey," Beulah said.

"I just gotta go to the men's room, then. I'll be right back." Wang did a perfect jeté accompanied by a rebel yell as Peter and Dick headed for the exit.

Behind the drop of the Hollywood Hills, J.O. was more sexually excited than he had ever been in his life, and he knew *exactly* what he had to do. Replacing the pencil stub in his notebook that now pictured drawings of various parts of the male anatomy, he crept away.

Putz, always slightly behind the others, was bending over tying his shoelace when he heard Beulah's whisper, "She likes Chinese but I'm a Tex/Mex kinda dame." Feeling her hand stealing up from behind, he bolted.

⌒⊃

In the dusty carpentry shop, J.O. found the wall rack with perfectly arranged tools. Too short to reach the brace and bit, he spied a wooden box to climb on.

⌒⊃

On stage, the dancers' disrespectful talk plus the ugly scene by that horrible child had unsettled Pittsburgh. Who the hell was he? Heading backstage to talk to Mona, he saw Nick and Suzie coming from the other side.

"My God!" Nick said, looking back toward the dressing room, "What legs!"

He was speaking English! Pittsburgh stepped quickly behind a dead-hung velour masking curtain.

"Do you think it's safe to drop the Italian?" Suzie asked.

"How could she forget that De Koven directed her in *Made in Orleans*? De Koven *made* her."

"I wouldn't be a bit surprised," Suzie said.

Pittsburgh's breath involuntarily imploded in a loud wheeze.

Both Suzie and Nick turned toward the drop.

"Did you hear something?" Suzie asked.

Coming up the steps from the basement, J.O. saw Suzie and Nick and quickly sidled behind the protective drop of the Hollywood Hills.

"Must be my imagination," Suzie said.

"Old theatres are mysterious," Nick said.

"They say they have ghosts."

Nick once again focused on the off stage portable dressing room. "They love her, don't they?"

"The crew?" Suzie asked.

"The crew, musicians, electrics, sound, costumes, wigs and hair, that pillow plumper and me."

"She's a pretty awful person," Suzie said.

"Last of the great stars."

"Good."

Nick looked questioningly.

"Didn't you see the way she treated her son?"

"Son?"

"J.O."

"What gave you the idea he's her son?" Nick asked.

"He called her mother."

"She never had any children."

"Oh, Nick! Why do you think he's called J.O.?"

"Because he's a jerk-off."

"J.O! Look about you. J.O. North Square. Does that clue you in to anything?"

"You think . . . ?"

"Of course."

Nick thought a moment.

"And that caricature, Beulah. Not only an insult to every black woman, she's a sadist. Look at the way she treats the boy."

Nick smiled. "Lighten up."

"April East is a monster."

Behind the velour, Pittsburgh held his breath so as not to make a sound.

"The daughter of Russian emigrants," Nick said, "she pulled herself up by her. . ."

". . .bra straps. The problem with that land-of-equal-opportunity idea is that everyone isn't equal."

"Certainly not in the chest department," Nick kidded as he headed for the stage door.

"And not everyone makes it."

"She did," Nick said.

"Most don't," Suzie said.

"But the opportunity is there."

"Only if you're ruthless enough, greedy enough, or if you have money power and influence to start with."

"You sound like my buddy Dean," Nick said, opening the stage door and admitting an acetylene-like shaft of light from the outside.

Brace and bit in hand, J.O. surveyed the back of the portable dressing room, which at first glance seemed insurmountable until he noticed the aluminum step ladder propped against the theatre's side wall. Once in place, he climbed on spindly, old man's legs, securing a position on the roof while he fitted the bit into the brace.

April East, as sexually apprehensive as a cat on a hot tin roof, was wiping the perspiration from her wrists and neck when something dropped into her cold cream jar. She examined it. Sawdust! "Fucking termites!" she said, swiping it out with a Kleenex tissue.

There was no alley leading to the street as is the case with New York theatres. Instead, the stage door Nick opened led directly into the west side of J.O. North Square, now a street fair. The whole county was present; hell, the whole world. Venders were everywhere: chili dogs, hot tamales, ears of red corn, posters of April East in her various roles.

Nick stopped to watch the painting of a T-shirt. The man was in his early twenties, thin and pockmarked. The painting was of a curvy April East wrapped in bunting holding the Statue of Liberty torch. Entwining her were masses of grapevines.

"You're good," Nick said. "What . . . tribe are you from?"

"Mandan."

"I don't think I've heard of them."

"Smallpox destroyed most of my ancestors. Now I count myself with the Arikara and Hidatsa, who are also disappearing. It was the Mandan who claimed that they climbed from beneath the earth on roots of grapevines."

"Perhaps they will again," Suzie said.

Nick examined a T-shirt which pictured an Indian profile, war paint over the lower half of the face, the upper half a crimson red. The hair was long and seemed to be blown clock-wise by the wind. Surrounding the profile were bird feathers rotating in a counter clockwise motion and beneath, a dark unknown—an abstraction—also in a curve.

"What does it mean?" Nick asked.

"Power comes from the circle. The circle is sacred, if it remains unbroken."

"How much?" Nick asked.

"Twenty-five bucks."

⌒⊙

Pittsburgh had extricated himself from the folds of the velour drop when he saw Mona hurrying out of the costume shop. "Psssst!"

"Why, what on earth . . . ! You startled me, Luv. Sent cold chills right up my spine."

"He speaks English!"

"Who?" Mona asked.

"Nicola Battisti Andreotti Sabbatini! That fake!" Looking around to see if anyone was lurking about, Pittsburgh drew Mona downstage. It was while their backs were turned that Wang, crossing the stage in the direction of the portable dressing room, executed a jeté and disappeared into the wing.

Downstage Pittsburgh scoffed. "He-men. HA! *They're* not exactly as they present themselves either!" He imploded a breath. "And *they* talk about *her*!"

"Who, Luv?" Mona asked.

"Miss East. I heard them! Saying the most outrageous things! An absolute calumny!"

"Calumny?"

"Lies! I was in high school when all that stuff came out about Bill Clinton, and next Obama and then after the Constitution was amended it started all over again and it goes on and on. I doubt it will ever change!" Pittsburgh's voice was strident. All this had been bottled up inside him for a long time.

Mona was perplexed. "What did they say about Ms. East?"

"It all started years ago with that trash about the President and First Lady in a ménage à trois with the Queen!"

"Well the *Enquirer* said they did."

"I am so tired of the slander, the gossip, tearing everything, every*one* down, like what they did to Ashton and Demi, just because she's twenty years older."

"I know, Luv, they want to destroy everything."

"Our most sacred institutions."

"What'd they say about Ashton?" Mona asked somewhat hastily.

Neither Mona nor Pittsburgh heard Beulah approach and her harsh voice startled them. "You seen Mistuh J.O.?"

"I haven't seen him since you *helped* him off stage after she took that spill," Mona said. "I just looked in the costume shop but he wasn't there, so naturally, I thought he was with you."

"I'll check her dressing room," Beulah said.

⌒↺

Inside the dressing room, Wang and April East's bodies were locked together in a deep tongue-sucking kiss. April was now in a state of extreme agitation, conscious only of her pounding heart and surging blood as she thrust her hand into his fly.

Through the hole he'd created in the roof J.O. gazed down and saw it all.

Beulah was about to knock on the Winnebago's door when she heard the heavy breathing. Putting her ear to the door she listened, withdrew, and had turned back on stage when she saw a strange distorted shadow spilling on the theatre's side wall. Something was jutting out over the dressing room's roof. Easing her way around to the back, she noticed the aluminum ladder and climbed it. The first thing she saw as her red bandanna-ed head appeared over the edge was the brace and bit. Crawling forward cautiously, she slammed her hand over J.O.'s mouth and pulled him away from the hole. Then, before he was conscious of what hit him, she put her eye to the shaft of yellow light and saw April East fellate Wang and then suddenly with one quick grasp, he ripped off her panties and spread her legs.

Rolling over on her back, Beulah pulled J.O. onto her ample body and propelled herself toward the ladder. She was descending, one hand still over J.O.'s mouth, his arms and legs flaying, when he bit her. He bit her on the exact spot, the fleshy part of her hand near the beginning of the thumb, as he had that morning. Crying out in pain she dropped him. He fell to the floor and in an instant was on his feet and running.

What had just happened inside was disastrous and could give away the whole game. In her effort to weaken April's influence, she had gone too far in urging her on. But how was she to know that the stupid bitch would lose her head? There would be repercussions. She had inadvertently jeopardized all she had worked for. Something had to be done. In a panic, she looked up and saw the old painted drop.

She quickly grabbed the single-edged razor blade that Pittsburgh used to 'distress' material in the costume shop. Back on stage, she moved the step ladder to the brick wall and climbed rapidly. Having reached the cat walk, she turned to the iron ladder attached to the wall which led into the fly loft. From there she could see that the heavy old drop she had seen from below was dead, hung from the fly gallery's beams since East's acting days in Timbuckone. It was held by three lines.

From high above the stage she looked down through the webbing of two-by- fours that formed the floor of the fly gallery and saw the door of the portable dressing room open and Wang emerge. She quickly cut the stage left line. As she did so, she saw Wang shaking his head as if stunned. As she moved quickly from left to right on the grid, and trying not to look down between the open spaces in the flooring, she bent and cut the lines. Now the drop, precariously sagging on either side, was suspended only by the center line. She saw that Wang was putting on his T-shirt. She became dizzy and knew that she had to hurry. At the center of the fly gallery, she reached with trembling hands through the space between the beam flooring and sliced the last rope. Standing, she moved quickly to the iron ladder and started her descent. But wait! Why hadn't she heard the crash? She looked out over the fly space. The old drop was suspended by only a single rope and Wang was dressed and about to cross the stage. My God! It couldn't remain hanging with all that weight! The rope *had* to give.

Below, Pittsburgh was telling Mona about how his assistant at Lay RòthChîld Film Studios had constantly been gossiping. As he recounted a tabloid article that claimed that a Supreme Court justice had had an affair with a famous female rock star, he heard a strange sound like wind in a sail, although he had never sailed in his life. Turning upstage, he saw Wang cross toward the stage door. Then, letting his eyes follow the sense of his ears, he looked up.

Grabbing Mona, he pulled her downstage so quickly that she lost her balance and fell on top of him. And so it was from the floor that he watched as the old drop came hurtling down. Broken wood, paint, dust, rose like debris from a tornado. My God, he thought, would it ruin the Ravenworld setting? His pillows?

When the dust had started to settle, he extricated himself from beneath the zaftig Mona and helped her to her feet.

"Wang! Wang!" Pittsburgh called, attempting to find him amidst the debris. Hearing a groan, he ripped away the torn canvas and cradled Wang's head in his lap as Mona held his hand.

"I . . . went . . . to . . ." Wang could barely talk.

"Yes. Yes. You went to . . . ?" Pittsburgh repeated.

"Miss East's . . . dressing room."

"Yes? Yes? Is she all right?" Pittsburgh asked.

"All right. Yes. Only . . ."

"Only . . . ?" Pittsburgh pressed Wang's hand urgently.

"Only she's . . ."

"What?" Mona asked.

"What? What?" Pittsburgh asked.

"Ohhhhhhh," Wang moaned, "Rrrrrrrrrrr, wwwwwwwwww," and went into convulsions.

"Wang! Wang!"

"Oh, my God! Luv." Mona pumped his hand.

"Wang, Wang," Pittsburgh cried, placing his head to the dancer's chest.

"Is he all right?" Mona asked. "Is he going to live?"

In a moment Pittsburgh raised his head. "He's dead."

"Dead?" Mona gasped.

"Dead!"

"How do you know?" Mona asked.

"His heart's stopped and he's not breathing."

Mona wrung her hands. "Oh, my God, my God!"

Pittsburgh knew instinctively that he had to comfort Mona. "Death be not proud," he said, remembering the way Brent Carver had said it on the Tony's a few years back. "Now what?"

"Now what? What?" Mona asked.

"What about the show? The show's *got* to go on!"

Mona groaned. "What are we going to do? Where are they going to find a Chinese/American muscle-man dancer in Timbuckone, North Dakota?"

A sudden idea slowly emerged in Pittsburgh's feverish brain. "Wait a minute," he said. "What about Wang's twin brother?"

"But . . . can he dance?"

"I don't know. We'll have to ask him. Come on." He grabbed her hand. "We've got to find out if Dong can dance!"

Backstage, one of the IATSE stagehands looked at the wreckage on stage and then crossed back, sat, and said to his fellow card players, "It was the old Cleon Throckmorton drop."

"This game is spit in the ocean."

"Ante up!"

Chapter X

Pittsburgh was stunned when he and Mona stepped outside. There had been a few gawkers in J.O. North Square that morning at 8:30 when he came to work but nothing to anticipate this bizarre bazaar. He hadn't seen anything like it since when in front of New York's Metropolitan Museum entrepreneurs hawked T-shirts for twenty-five bucks bearing the face of Osama bin Laden and below, a simple quintessential Americanism, "We Gotcha! Rag-head!"

Here in J.O. Square it was April East 'Torso' T-shirts with grotesquely enlarged breasts, a stud cowpoke type with an Alfred E. Newman expression on his sexually satiated face, and a thought cloud, reading, "I was in Timbuckone with April East and survived." Another silk screened imprint of April showed vivid red lips parted, ready to insert a peeled-back banana, "Potassium be damned! I'd rather eat a . . . ." Venders were selling green foam-rubber spiked April-East-as-Miss- Liberty crowns of red, white and blue and Miss Liberty 'flashlights' with light coming from both nipples. Near the east end of the Square, a tent housed a portable bar over which hung an enormous painting of April, a la *September Morn*. A caption underneath read: "Suck on a Grand Teton at the biggest bar in the world."

The high school band played John Philip Sousa's "Stars and Stripes Forever," badly, while pudgy drum majorettes in red, white, and blue scanty attire, their heads crowned with red fright wigs to make them resemble April East, twirled batons.

"The utter *commerce* of it all!" Pittsburgh lamented. "There's no other word for this. It's simply soul-destroying."

"You mustn't expect too much of people, Luv," Mona warned him as they hurried on, "or they'll be sure to disappoint you."

⌒○

In Wang's room, Mona held the stricken Dong in a tight embrace and patted his back. "We're terribly sorry to be the ones to have told you," Pittsburgh said, "and I know it may sound inappropriate, coming just after you've lost your brother, but can you dance?"

"Yes," Dong said.

"Do you think you could go on in Wang's place?"

Dong wiped his eyes with the Kleenex Mona provided from her clutch bag. "Is OK," he said. "Grateful for opportunity in America."

"We've already checked with Peter, the dance captain. He'll fill you in on anything you need to know," Pittsburgh said. "And try to be brave. Just remember what Buddha. . ."

"I know," Dong said. "He teach us that suffering is inseparable from existence."

"Or as we say in America, 'the show must go on,'" Mona said.

⌒○

"It's the Chinese who have the get-up-and-go of the Protestant work ethic," Pittsburgh observed as he and Mona left the hotel's elevator and headed for Ms. East's room.

"But, Luv, aren't most of them Buddhist?" Mona asked.

"I'm not sure," Pittsburgh said shifting the flowers from his arm and tapping at the door. "Yoo-hoo? Anyone home? Yoo-hoo!" he called. "Yoo-hoo? Yoooooooo-hoooooo? Miss East?"

There was no answer.

"You suppose she's downstairs in the dining room?"

"I doubt it, Luv. She doesn't eat out," Mona said.

"Let me just drop off these flowers." He placed the key firmly in the lock.

"You don't think she'll mind, Luv?" Mona asked as the door opened.

"She *loves* orange blossoms. And I ordered enough for both the set and here. This won't take a sec."

༄

April East's private suite on the seventh floor, now in semi-darkness, was dressed as an exact replica of her gold, white, and mirrored salon at Ravenworld. This "real" room was designed to reinforce the theatrically of the setting on stage. Pittsburgh went directly to the piano and put the flowers in the Ming vase, pausing to snip the odd wilted petal and remove buds that did not suit his standard of freshness. In the meantime, Mona examined the decor. "Fab, fab, *fab*-u-lous!" she inhaled.

"Like it?" Pittsburgh asked.

"It's *exactly* like the set!"

"It does have a certain verisimilitude."

Looking through the Tudor windows at the painted backdrop, Mona said, "Looks exactly like the HOLLYWOOD sign used to look: whitewashed against dead grass."

"Rigging the backdrop in here was not easy," Pittsburgh admitted, plucking another dead bud. "But I insisted because I wanted her to be reminded of her Hollywood Studio. But it was hard since Sparks had only five feet of throw for the lighting."

"Looks absolutely real," Mona said after Pittsburgh turned the knob on the rheostat that brought up the lights on the Hollywood Hills drop.

"The space back here is so jerry-rigged you wouldn't believe! Stage Right is a dead end."

Mona looked Stage Left.

"No! Stage *Right*." Pittsburgh pointed.

"Have patience, Luv."

"Women and their sense of direction! But there *is* an exit that leads to the back stairs that's Stage Left!"

Mona looked vaguely in the direction he was pointing.

After adding a packet of "flower fresh" to the water, he gave the room one last inspection. "Well, we might as well be on our way. I should check the cleaning crew's work and see if they've gotten rid of all that dust." But at the door he could not resist stopping and turning back for one last look at his handiwork. "While I was working here, making this ugly square room into an exact replica of her studio in Hollywood, I got this feeling . . ."

"What, Luv?" Mona asked. She added when Pittsburgh did not respond immediately, "Luv, you're making cold shivers run right up my spine!"

"Of what it must be like to see things through her eyes, to *be* her."

"How could anyone *be* someone else?"

He knew it was futile to try to explain. As he stood there transfixed, in deep meditation, there came the sudden sound of running feet in the hallway followed by a struggle.

"You can't go in there!" Beulah shouted.

"I'm going to see Mother!" J.O. screamed.

Pittsburgh looked around frantically. In the hall, there was further commotion and someone grabbed the door knob and the door started to open but was slammed shut. Galvanized into action, Pittsburgh indicated the window seat. "We'll just go down the back stairs."

"Mama! Mama!" J.O. yelled out in the hall.

"Hush your mouth. Ain't gonna do no good you callin' yo Mama," Beulah said. "She don't want to see you. You know she don't. Now you come along wid me."

Opening the Tudor windows, Pittsburgh stepped over the window seat and turned to help Mona.

"Mama!"

"No good you callin' yo Mama," Beulah said. "You know you ain't *ever* allowed in her rooms."

"Stage left, to the back stairs," Pittsburgh directed. But in her effort to quickly traverse the window seat, Mona had inadvertently upset a pillow which fell onto the floor.

"I want an audience with Mama. I'm gonna tell her you slapped me."

While Pittsburgh reached for the pillow, the hall door swung open. He quickly dropped to the floor behind the window unit, hoping that he hadn't been seen.

Inside the room, Beulah struggled to get J. O. back into the hall.

Crawling stage left toward the back staircase, Pittsburgh had not moved two feet before he realized what had happened. Mona had gone in the wrong direction. He turned and motioned for her to stay where she was. In the room, J.O. tore himself from Beulah, ran to the piano, attached himself to its leg and screamed, "Mama! Mama!"

"Hush your mouth! Yo Mama ain't gonna wanta see you ever again after what you done up on the roof of her dressing room!"

"I didn't see nothin'. Honest I didn't."

"You know you ain't suppose to tote paper and pencil and write things." Beulah gave a twist to his leg.

At J.O.'s wail, Pittsburgh peeked out and saw Beulah grab J.O.'s notebook. He motioned for Mona to cross over to his side. But before she could, a voice came from behind the door to the room's interior. "For God's sake what is all the commotion?"

Beulah wrenched J.O. from the piano's leg and yanked him to his feet.

The door inside the room flew open and a figure in black, an ancient withered crone, barely skin and bones, rolled into the room in a wheelchair, a box in her lap and a silver cane beside her. "What in God's name is all this commotion?" The Old Woman repeated, louder this time.

"Get back, get back!" Beulah hissed.

"What do you mean 'get back'? What in hell is going on?"

Encased between Beulah's gigantic breasts, J.O was suffocating. And as oft happens with those close to death, he was given an extra surge of energy, enough to wrench himself free. Once he had sucked in the life-giving air, he screamed, "Mama!" but the scream stopped in his mouth. He stared at The Old Woman, then turned in confusion to Beulah, whose eyes were rolled upward in her head.

"Sweet Jesus!" she muttered. "Now what?"

"Who's she?" J.O. asked, pointing to The Old Woman.

"How did he get in here?" the woman asked.

"The door was unlocked!" Beulah answered.

"Who unlocked it?"

"I don't know," Beulah said. "*Now what?*"

"Don't lose your head!" The Old Woman said with great authority.

J.O. drew near. "Who are you? Why are you in Mama's apartment?"

The Old Woman smiled. "She invited me, dear. You see we're . . . we're very old friends." Beulah moved away and shook her head with a what-in-hell-are-we-gonna-do-now expression on her broad face. "You might as well know, dear. I'm your Aunt Nellie. Your mother's sister."

"She never had a sister," J.O. said ruefully.

"There were two—twins—but one was stillborn."

"Mama was so much younger and you are so . . . old," J.O. said. "Mama didn't want anyone to know she had a sister so old, didn't want anyone to *see* you."

"You're a regular Sherlock Holmes."

Beulah held out the spiral notebook for The Old Woman's inspection.

"It's not my writing, Aunt Nellie!"

The Old Woman read the infantile printing silently until reaching: "She unzipped his pants and Wang was trying to get his hand between her legs and . . ."

"What is this?" The Old Woman demanded of Beulah.

"Well, Miss Nellie," Beulah said, "I done found Master J.O. with a brace and bit. He had made a hole, this big"—she made a circle with her thumb and index finger—"on top of his Mama's dressing room."

"Had he . . . ?"

"I didn't do nothin'!" J.O. yelled.

Beulah looked through the circle made by her thumb and index finger. "Yes you did!"

"No, I did not!" J.O. screamed.

"Quiet!" The Old Woman commanded and turned to Beulah. "Was she. . ?"

"Yes," Beulah said.

"How do you know?"

"I looked."

"And she was . . . ?"

"*He* was!" Beulah pointed to the notebook, "Exactly what's written."

The Old Woman clenched her teeth and shook her head.

"She was in heat, out of control, his paws all over her. He ran his hand down, then froze, like he'd touched a hot poker."

The Old Woman brightened perceptibly, "A hot pecker?"

"A hot *poker*!"

"Well, learn to enunciate, Liver Lips!" After a silence, The Old Woman said, "If he knows, we've got to *get* to Wang."

"I already did," Beulah said.

"How?"

"Not in front of the kid."

The Old Woman spit out the words. "Fuck the kid!"

Pittsburgh raised his head and peered into the room.

"What did you say?" J.O. asked.

"I said, 'fuck you, kid,'" The Old Woman snarled. "Now, shut up!"

"How dare you talk to me like that."

Wheeling herself close to J.O., The Old Woman reached out her left hand and slapped him, sending him sprawling to the floor.

Pittsburgh's mind reeled as he connected the dots. It was the exact action from *Made in Orleans* when April East was holding out her left hand to Basil Rathbone as Pontius Pilot. The Old Woman had slapped J.O.'s *right* cheek with the palm of her right hand! Pittsburgh felt the goose bumps rising. The Old Woman was . . . double jointed! There was no doubt about it!

He ducked back behind the window seat.

"How did you get rid of Wang?" The Old Woman asked.

Beulah gave a not-in-front-of-the-kid head-shake in J.O.'s direction. "There was an accident."

"What kind?"

"An industrial accident. An old drop plummeted from the flies. Lines frayed."

"Frayed?"

Beulah reached into her pocket and held out Pittsburgh's 'distress' razor.

"Is he . . ."

"Yes."

"Instantly?"

"Almost."

"Then it wasn't instantly!"

"No."

"Did he talk?"

"I'm not sure."

"Who was there?"

"That fool pillow plumper and Mona."

Pittsburgh and Mona exchanged a look behind the window seat.

"Did he tell them?"

"I don't know!" Beulah yelled.

The Old Woman raised her cane. "Don't you *ever* raise your voice to me!" Then after a moment, she added, "We've got to find out if Wang talked to those two."

"It doesn't matter if he did."

"What do you mean it doesn't matter?"

"I'll take care of them!" Beulah made a gesture of slitting her throat.

Four deaths in the same day? Pittsburgh wondered from behind the French window.

"I'm going to get rid of . . ." The Old Woman nodded in the direction of J.O.

In the silence that followed, Pittsburgh counted on his fingers: one was for Wang, two was for J.O . . . He looked at Mona who would be three and he would be . . .

A key was heard turning in the room's door. From the hotel's corridor there was a distinct, "Goddamn it!" followed by the key turning in the lock once again. The door swung open. Seeing The Old Woman and Beulah, April East was shocked. Then seeing J.O, she realized something had gone terribly wrong.

"My *nephew*, J.O, dear *sister*," The Old Woman said, giving the introduction a moment to sink in, "apparently peeked into your dressing room."

The pause was only momentary. "How do you mean?"

"Did you *do* what I explicitly told you *never* to do again? Did you?"

April East looked at Beulah. If she had said something about Wang, how much did she tell?

The Old Woman turned to J.O. "Dear?"

"Yes, Aunt Nellie?"

"Do you have to go to the bathroom?"

"Yes! Yes!" He turned to April East. "Would it be all right, Mama?"

"Sure, Kid. Go to the toilet," April spat. "Take as long as you like!"

J.O. skipped happily to the door and exited into the corridor.

"Lock him in," The Old Woman said to Beulah. "I'll take care of him later."

"Well," she asked April when they were alone, "do you deny Beulah's story?"

"Which was?" April asked.

"The dancer was *in* and you were *out* of control."

"All right, cards on the table. Wang did come to my dressing room. The boy had been coming on to me all through rehearsals. He said today that he wanted to see me. I thought it was about the act, but then when he came in and started making advances I gave him his walking papers."

The Old Woman smiled. "Is that all you gave him?"

"Absolutely!"

"Beulah says you gave a little more."

"How would Beulah know?"

"You deny it?"

"I do deny it! That's *not* what happened. Beulah hates me. She's always hated me."

"Why do you say that?" The Old Woman asked.

"She's afraid that after you . . ."

"Yes?"

". . . pass, I'll be running the show."

"I suspected a power struggle after my death," The Old Woman said with a bemused smile.

"But even if it did happen—which *it did not*—Wang is dead. I saw the body when I left the theatre."

"Yes, he's dead, thanks to Beulah. But prior to dying he *may* have talked!"

"To who?" April asked.

"To *whom*!" The Old Woman snarled.

"Sorry."

"Mona and that pillow plumper!"

Both Pittsburgh and Mona looked out cautiously.

April considered this possibility before she spoke. "How do you know?"

"Then it *did* happen!" The Old Woman said.

"No!" April answered quickly, too quickly she realized. "I told you, nothin' happened." And then, looking back at the door she added, "How does Beulah know Wang said anything?"

"She doesn't."

"Well, there, you see?"

"But I can't take any chances!"

At that moment the hall door opened and Beulah returned.

"Did you lock him in?" The Old Woman asked.

"Yes, he's happy as a clam."

"I'll decide later how to get rid of him."

"If we leave him there long enough he could . . ." Beulah moved her fist rapidly in short strokes, ". . . himself to death!" She laughed and whipped off her red bandanna and wig, "If you ask me . . ."

"No one has," The Old Woman shot back.

"The sooner we get rid of J.O. the better," Beulah said. She stripped off her blouse, reached up in back and unhooked the brassiere. Releasing her arms from the white straps, she tossed the brassiere with its two gigantic foam rubber breasts onto the window seat. "I'll take care of those other two," he said, scratching the hair on his muscular black chest.

Pittsburgh and Mona ducked, but heard The Old Woman sigh.

"The little bastard bit me," Beulah growled, sucking on the fleshy part of his hand. "Mona didn't watch him like she was supposed to and I can't do that all the time *and* watch over her." He pointed in the direction of April. "And be houseboy to you."

"You haven't been much of a 'houseboy' to me for a long time," The Old Woman said.

"Hah!" April taunted. "It's a little hard to . . ."

"Not *hard* enough!" The Old Woman snapped.

Attempting to shift the focus from himself, Beulah turned to April. "You blew it, baby, you blew it again."

"You lie," April spat.

"Oh, no! You got that Chink hunk in your dressing room and gave head until the slant wanted it the old fashioned way and you were so carried away."

"OK, cards on the table," April said to The Old Woman. "You want to know what happened? This bastard tried to set me up. He came to my dressing room, actually suggested that he solicit one of the muscle boys for me."

"That's a lie!" Beulah said stepping out of his skirt.

"No it isn't. Once a pimp, always a pimp," April said.

"Fuck you, bitch!"

"Don't you wish you could!"

Beulah's fist shot out and connected squarely with April's jaw, decking her. As she fell, her red hair flew off.

"You bastard!" she screamed, charging Beulah, fists in the air.

Pittsburgh and Mona looked on in horror.

"Stop it! Stop it!" The Old Woman commanded, her cane pointed at them. "Nothing will be solved by breaking his jaw, you ass! Now sit down. Both of you."

They sat.

Chapter XI

Pittsburgh was stunned to have heard The Old Woman refer to April in the masculine gender.

"I'm upset with both of you," The Old Woman said, adding with bitter resignation, "you can dress 'em up but you can't take 'em out!" She pointed to Beulah. "You're responsible for J.O. Yes, I let you talk me into hiring Mona to help you keep him out of the way, but I told you at the time that the responsibility was still yours. You blew it!" She turned to April. "And as for your disgusting display this morning with that 'who do you have to fuck around here' entrance, I would *never* have used that cheap line. Right out of your Kansas City trailer-park backyard. I knew when I first met you that you were a vulgarian."

"I admit I lost it when that chair . . ."

"You reverted to type. But that's blood under the bridge. Now let's get back to business. Beulah *saw* you from the roof where a hole had been bored. Now for the last time, did you . . . ?"

"I got carried away, once in how many years?"

"Twice!" The Old Woman raged.

April looked as though he might protest but The Old Woman cut him off. "Don't pretend you don't remember Las Vegas!" She paused for her words to sink in. "Your shenanigans there forced me back into retirement just as my career had revived."

"I never thought that guy would try to rape me," April said. "None of the others . . . they were all satisfied—eager—to do it my way."

"Oh, give me a break!" Beulah said.

"Try to understand," April said, pleading with The Old Woman. "I've been without a man for such a long time."

"Welcome to the real world!" The Old Woman said.

"It was just a moment of passion."

"I've told you a thousand times, passion is profoundly dangerous," The Old Woman bellowed. "You'll have to take the consequences!"

Beulah smiled. "Five deaths?"

Behind the window seat, Pittsburgh shuddered.

"Five!" The Old Woman shot back.

Removing a small bottle of medicine from his purse, April placed it on the end table next to the Louis Seize sofa. He was becoming warmer as the panic grew. He removed his blouse and then released the brassiere along with the straps that pulled his silicone breasts together to give the effect of cleavage. He did all this slowly as he talked, trying desperately to calm himself. "What harm is done? Wang is dead."

The Old Woman saw the beads of perspiration form on his brow. He was always weak, she thought. He had told her that he'd had rheumatic fever as a boy, leaving him with a bad heart, which right now was going a mile a minute. A smile spread over her wrinkled face. *Maybe nature would take care of what had to be done.*

As his panic increased and the heart beat became faster and more erratic, April put his hand on his neck to feel the pulse. "You see," he said slowly to calm himself, "I was so . . . in love."

"Love!" The Old Woman laughed. "It wasn't love. You were hot!"

"Love!" April said. Then trying to calm himself, he added, "Needing it so that there came a point when it didn't matter any longer what I was. He was so gentle, so passionate. I thought my being, the way I was born, wouldn't matter to him."

"Wouldn't matter?" Beulah said contemptuously. "Get real, slut!"

"Shut up!" The Old Woman commanded. She wheeled her chair back and forth and muttered to herself, "If Wang told Mona and that pillow plumper and they've talked, we're in major trouble."

"Chances are he didn't," April said. "I think we should just go on with the taping as though nothing happened."

The Old Woman continued thinking as she moved back and forth in her chair. "You may be right. Maybe he didn't."

"I'm sure he didn't," April said.

"But even if he didn't, it's only dumb, blind luck. You're not to be trusted. You made a major mistake, twice!"

April could feel the panic, the increased heart rate. "I'm sorry," he said.

"Sorry is not enough," The Old Woman said.

"It will never happen again, I promise."

"You promised me the same thing last time. So what to do?"

"Another female impersonator?" Beulah suggested. "They're a dime a dozen."

"True, impersonators *are* a dime a dozen. But that's not what we're talking about, idiot! What I need is someone who has the talent to *become* the other."

Pittsburgh heard it all from behind the window seat and knew that she was right.

"When I was young," The Old Woman said, "there was what we called 'star quality.' Each star was unique: voice, gestures, movement, mannerisms. So I asked myself, 'What if I stole all those uniquenesses and combined them into one?' MINE. ME!" She paused for a moment to stroke a long black hair growing from her chin. "It won't be easy to find a replacement. Becoming another is difficult. Mannerisms are not the same thing. They are only the external wrapping. Style must be approached from within. *Why* does a person do what she does? Why that manner of smoking, that way of speaking, that way of carrying the head, that way of smiling? All these characteristics come from *inside*. If they don't, it's just mimicry. To become, you have to get inside *the mind* of the person being imitated. ME!" Again she tugged at the single black hair as she looked at April. "You were very good at that. Yes, you were."

April gasped at the use of the past tense.

"Over time, you *became* the sum of all the uniqueness I had observed in others. They became *you*!"

What The Old Woman put into words was what Pittsburgh had always known. Since he was a kid, he had needed to be someone else. His true identity was not that of a male set dresser. His true identity was that of a great female star, an April East! It had always been thus. Swept away by the idea, he rose. "You're April East, aren't you?" he said to The Old Woman.

Beulah, April and The Old Woman turned toward the window seat in astonishment as Mona tugged at Pittsburgh's sleeve in an effort to hush him.

The silence that followed his revelation was finally broken by The Old Woman. "How long have you been here?"

"From the beginning," Pittsburgh answered.

"Then you heard it all?"

"Yes, Miss East."

The Old Woman turned to April. "Truthfulness," she observed. She then turned back and said, "You called me Miss East."

Pittsburgh stepped over the window seat into the room. "Yes."

"How did you know?"

Pittsburgh gave a quick pantomimed demonstration of the slap The Old Woman had given J.O.

The Old Woman smiled in recognition.

Going to the piano, Pittsburgh selected a few stems and placed the orange blossoms in her lap. "I bought these especially for you."

"Thank you." She smiled. He give a slight bow, backed up three paces.

"They were always my favorite."

"At first I thought you were your mother," he said. "But I knew that was impossible because I read of her death . . . your world tour . . . the fiery plane crash over the Himalayas."

"You seem to know everything about . . . Miss East."

"The courage it must have taken! Spending those nights in 'frozen hell' as the tabloid headlines read, walking thirty miles through the blizzard, living on—I never believed those stories."

"The *Enquirer* said the most awful things," Mona explained.

"I figured out what you ate," Pittsburgh said. And in answer to The Old Woman's quizzical look he said, "Dried yak."

"No, the *Enquirer* was right. It was mother!"

For an instant the conditioned taboo against cannibalism filled Pittsburgh's Catholic alter-boy conscience. Then after a moment he rationalized. "Well, *you survived!*"

"It makes no difference to you if the real April East is old?"

"None!" Pittsburgh said.

"Of course not, Luv!" Mona chimed in.

"You're not members of our throw-away society?"

"I would have known at once!" Pittsburgh said. "Except for the speech. You talk different in real life."

The Old Woman put her hands on her hips as she did a perfect imitation of the star's innuendo-filled, aspirate voice. "How'd you like me to talk, Cowboy?"

"Amazing!" Pittsburgh said.

"No one talks that way in real life," The Old Woman interrupted, followed by an enormous sneeze.

"Here, let me take those." As Pittsburgh put the flowers back in the Ming vase, The Old Woman looked at Beulah and shook her head. "Seems like such a nice boy, it's a pity . . ."

Pittsburgh turned from the piano where he was now tidying up the sheet music. "Pity?"

"You came in so precipitously and overheard us," The Old Woman said and shrugged. "Well, these things happen. Can't be helped. Ayn Rand was right. Objectivism/Sympathy must remain out of all business transactions. The only thing is . . . I hate to dispatch a fan."

"Dispatch?" Pittsburgh asked.

"I was using the word in the Elizabethan sense, dear."

"She means kill." Beulah smiled.

"Nothing personal," The Old Woman added.

"Of course not," Pittsburgh said hoarsely as he and Mona sank onto the piano bench.

The Old Woman turned her attention back to April and Beulah. "I retired from the stage so that *no* one would ever see me *old*. The myth would survive the deterioration of the body." She indicated her withered face. "I didn't want my public to see me as Maria Ouspenskaya—or whoever played that role—as she was coming out of Shangri La!"

Pittsburgh raised his hand

"Yes?" she asked.

"It was Margo. Her first picture." Then turning to Mona, he explained, "When Ronald Coleman brought Margo out of Shangri La, she was really seven hundred years old, and when she came into the outer world her face just *withered*! I mean, she just fell apart!"

"Uggers!" Mona said. "Makes cold chills run right up my spine, Luv."

"Yes, it was Margo," The Old Woman said. She turned to April. "If only you had the same sense of film history! Now, where was I?"

"You said," Pittsburgh chimed in, "you retired from the films so no one would ever see you *old*."

"You listen well," The Old Woman said. "No, I had not been seen for years, but then I got an offer to return to the stage and I began planning a new act and during that time Beulah the First—an aficionado of drag—talked me into visiting . . . .”

⌒⊃

A black stretch limo pulled up to the curb in front of a cheesy night club in New York City's West Village. A heavily veiled woman in black was helped out by Max, the chauffeur, followed by Beulah the First, wearing a suit.

The couple entered the small, smoky night club and were seated at a table in the rear of the room as the Master of Ceremonies announced, "And now, ladies and gentlemen, Club Ridiculous is proud to present . . . Horace Mann as the one and only, the incomparable . . . MIZZ APRIL EAST!" He was dressed and made up as the Star at the height of her fame. The audience went wild, not so much for the young performer as for the legend he was representing.

A handsome muscular man appeared wearing only a dance belt. A short musical intro was played establishing that the muscle man would be used as a prop. The song was sung with an emphasis on sexual innuendo in relation to the trophy boy.

> He seemed common as dirt
> A most ordinary squat
> I met him on the bus
> As it was travelin' west.
> That speckled tie
> That spot of pie
> I saw on his vest
> As the bus traveled west
> Distressed me. . .
> I now know why
> He turned out to be
> A most exceptional guy.
> And that ain't no lie

> Because he's . . .
> Well you can see . . .
> Because he's . . .
> Yummyyyyyy.

An elderly man sitting at a table directly in front of the Woman in Black and Beulah the First, tears streaming down his face, whispered, "My God, was there *ever* a star of East's magnitude?"

"And will there ever be one again?" his male companion replied . . . .

∽

The Old Woman broke from her reverie for a moment to explain.

"Circumstances: the bad relationship between you and your parents, your age, talent, and most of all, looks, along with the fact that I was going stir crazy in retirement and had been offered a very lucrative contract to appear at the Sands in Las Vegas. All of this offered up the perfect storm for the dispatching of your colleague, Danny. Naturally, a great deal of effort and planning had gone into the screening and surveillance before we saw you, but ironically it was a trifle, your Onyx Ring, that cinched the final decision: our selection of you as my stand-in on our first visit to view your act . . . ."

∽

Backstage at the Club, a young bare chested Horace was removing his makeup and Danny, another female impersonator, was at the mirror putting on his makeup in preparation for going on.

"Great house, tonight!" Horace enthused.

"I watched you. You were wonderful!"

"Thanks, Danny. They love you."

"Not as much as you. The order is all screwed up. I should be going on before you. Your act should get top billing. The way it is now, it's like the trained seals going on *after* Sophie Tucker!"

The Stage Manager opened the dressing room door. "Horace, there's a gentleman here to see you."

Horace looked at Danny. "OK by you if he comes in?"

"Hell, everyone in the world has seen all I got in my package."

"Please send him in."

The black man entered.

"Yes?"

"I work with Miss East."

"April East!"

"Yes, in cognate. We were in the audience tonight."

"Oh, I hope I didn't do anything to offend her. I wouldn't . . ."

"She loved your performance. As a matter of fact, she's out front in her limo and would very much like to meet you."

"Oh, my God!"

"May I go too?" Danny asked. "Just to say hello?"

"I think it best for you to wait," the gentleman said. "I'll broach the matter and if she consents, I'll come back and get you."

At the curb Beulah opened the limousine's door. Horace clasped a hand to his chest as he looked at his unveiled idol. He was near tears. "Miss East! This is the greatest honor in my life."

"Please come in."

Horace slid in beside her and Beulah took the jump seat.

"You were almost perfect," April East said. "Perhaps a little off here, a little off there, where the splices had not yet adhered, but *almost* perfect. You have penetrated my soul!"

Horace was overcome and started to cry. "Oh!"

East took his hand. "I will not waste your time or mine. I have had an offer to return to the stage. I have a brand new act very much in mind. Would you be interested?"

"Are you offering me a job?"

"Yes."

"Oh, my God! Yes, Yes, Yes! I would give my very soul to work with you."

East smiled. "Exactly what will be needed. That is, in addition to your talent. But would you be willing to give up everything? Even your own identity?"

"What do you mean?"

"As Horace Mann?"

"I would give that up, and a great deal more."

"I mean, would you *become* me?"

"For that chance, I would do anything you asked."

East took a moment and smiled, then looked at Beulah. "I don't see any point in putting this off any longer. Do you mind waiting here for a moment. No need to be frightened. Max, our chauffeur, is in the front seat."

"No! Anything you say. *Anything!*"

"I need to speak to Beulah for a moment. I can use some air. Oh, by the way, that unusual ring you're wearing." It was a large black onyx ring, surrounded by sparkling cut-glass diamonds, on the third finger of his right hand.

"It's just a junk piece of jewelry I made for myself."

It's very eye catching; two of the critics mentioned it in their reviews," April East said, holding out her hand palm- up.

"Then please, Miss East, May I give it to you?"

"Thank you. I'd like that."

❧

There was just the slightest trace of lower Manhattan fog surrounding The Woman in Black and Beulah the First as they whispered at the head of the alley.

"Then now!" she said angrily.

"Hold! Perhaps wait a week at least before the actual deed."

"You are too full of the milk of human kindness," she said. "We do it now just as we planned!"

"But what if he suspects?"

"Look innocent, but be the serpent underneath."

At the dressing room, Beulah rapped and opened the door. "Danny, she'll see you."

"Ohhhh, I'm so excited. Is it all right for me to meet her like this?" Danny asked, indicating his skimpy drag outfit. "I'm undressed to go on and I won't have time to redress and then undress again before . . . but I wouldn't miss this opportunity for anything."

"You're fine as you are. Lovely," he said, reaching out his hands to grab the boy's neck to strangle the scream.

When Danny was lifeless, Beulah picked up the body, checked the hallway, and headed for the stage door. The Woman in Black stood shrouded in fog at the end of the dimly lit alleyway. Beulah carried the nearly nude body to her. "More fight than I expected from one of his kind."

The dead face was wild with mascara streaked eyes, lipstick smeared mouth, face rouged against the milk white skin that accompanies death, the red wig askew, the padded bra hanging from one shoulder, all attesting to the struggle that had taken place in the dressing room. The Woman in Black slipped the onyx ring onto the corpse's right third finger, noting the fine line of dark hair running down over the young abs to a forest of black pubic hair. For just the fraction of a moment she had a gnawing sense of loss. Shaking it off, she twisted the ring to its proper position on his finger. "That should serve," she said. "Now do your thing."

As if desperate to rid himself of it, Beulah lifted the body over his head and with all his strength threw it onto the cobblestones where it began to bleed like a bloody rag. Beulah's breath came quickly. "Anything else?"

She smiled in anticipation. "There might be dental identification. If you could just. . ."

Beulah's boot crashed down on the face, over and over again, breaking in the mouth, battering out the teeth, the nose, the eyes, until all facial identity was erased. What remained was no more than a mangled, hollowed-out melon rind.

As they drove through the night, April East told Horace Mann of his friend's fate. She told it graphically to test his endurance and strength. "We killed him. His mangled body lies bleeding in the alley."

The horrified Horace tried desperately to remain calm. He was aware of his weak heart. What was happening to him was too much to contemplate. He would go mad. He almost broke when he whispered, "Do you know what will become of his body?"

The Old Woman seemed to take delight in the telling. "He will be discovered. New York's Finest will leave the body for a few weeks in the city medical examiner's office. You, Horace will not show up for your next performance. One of the drag queens will identify the body as you from the ring. Your parents will be notified, but they will be too ashamed to claim the body. There will be a burial in Potter's Field on Hart's Island with the city's unwanted in a mass grave. A priest will observe, indifferently. You see, the world hates men who are not real men. Now, on with the show and let us never speak of this again . . . ."

⌇⌇

The gasp of breath emanating from Horace's throat brought Pittsburgh back to the present.

"That is how April East was reborn," The Old Woman said. "The death of Danny Boy was insignificant, only a means to immortality in my future performances."

"*My* performances," Horace said.

"*I* survived! April East lived on."

"Through me."

"Yes, you," The Old Woman acknowledged.

"First I did the film," Horace said.

"*My* comeback," The Old Woman purred.

"Even Lee Strasberg—who had a cameo in the picture— couldn't tell. And then I did the stage play."

"My triumphant return to Broadway. And then another show at Vegas' Sands," The Old Woman said.

"*It was I,*" Horace cried out, "who was paid fifty thousand a show, more than Sinatra, more than Streisand, more than Madonna."

"And more than that . . . *Jennifer Lopez!*" The Old Woman spat out the name. "And I kept on going."

"Every day *I* rehearsed as you, what to do and what *not* to do."

"People couldn't believe how young *I* looked."

"How young I *was!*" Horace said.

"If *I* could remain young, so could they. They couldn't believe my legs."

"*My* legs!" Horace echoed.

Then with a ferocity that she had not displayed since the event occurred, The Old Woman bawled, "Then I was forced into retirement because of you and the Vegas incident . . . ."

It was Horace Mann as April East at the second gig at the Sands. The Old Woman was on top of the world. She had discarded the four muscle men she had used in her comeback and now had only one: a young guy, kinda shy, good lookin' and straight. Hiring him was her first mistake, for unbeknownst to her, Horace had fallen hard, and anyone who saw the act with this new young man could tell there was a difference in his performance. April East was in love.

> He's somethin' to look at
> Somethin' to see
> Just glad I'm livin'
> Happy to be
> I got a guy
> Crazy for me
> Crazy for me
> He's funny that way!

After the act, the bows taken, the applause and cheers received, Horace looked at himself in the dressing room mirror. He not only felt, but could see the change that love had wrought in him after years of excruciating hard work—"getting it right"—under the secret tutelage of The Woman in Black. At first it was easy because he so idolized her, but as time wore on, her driven, enforced perfectionism enslaved him.

Although he had been in sympathy with her aims, was it because they paralleled his own as an actor? Or was it the Patty Hearst-Stockholm syndrome of sympathizing with one's captor? Whatever the cause, he was no longer a slave to her demands. Love had freed him!

A knock on the door and there he was in all his youthful beauty. Without saying a word Horace/April took him in his arms, embraced him passionately, and suddenly they were locked in a deep kiss. In a state of extreme agitation, Horace lost all control as the young man's mouth touched his silicone breasts. Opening his fly and reaching inside sent a shock wave through Horace that he had never known.

The Young Man gently urged April into a chair, slid out of his trousers and thrust his pelvis toward her. As April fellated him, the boy began to moan, and reaching the height of passion, he closed his eyes and cried out, pumping and overflowing onto her. Spent, he sank to his knees, "Oh, God! That was the best I ever had, oh . . ." His voice trailed off as his eyes saw the jock strap. With a quick grasp, he lowered it, revealing the male genitalia. His mouth agape, he looked up in horror as though unable to comprehend and stumbled toward the door.

"What difference does the plumbing make?" Horace pleaded.

The boy's face turned ugly. "I'm not a fag!"

"But you said it was the best you ever had."

"You tricked me. . . . How could I . . . ?"

"But you did! So what difference does it make?"

"I'm not gay. I feel disgust!"

"No. Disgust is not what you felt."

"Just wait until your 'public' finds out."

"No! Please . . ."

"Keep this a secret? No way!"

The door of the dressing room had opened silently. The boy was hit from behind. He doubled up as he fell, writhing in agony. Horace's attention was riveted on his convulsing body. Then slowly he looked up to see The Woman in Black in the doorway, her silver cane raised; from it curled a faint trace of blue smoke.

The headlines screamed: "Vegas Stunned. Dancer Dies in April East's Dressing Room." "Foul Play Suspected." "East Claims Snake Bite." "Hearing Set."

April sat in the court dock in a stunning black dress, cut low in front and back, skirt slit up the side to reveal a leg. She confirmed her love for the young man and said that because of his death she would retire from the stage. The judge leaned over the bench, gazing down at her as though possessed.

In back, among the spectators, sat The Woman in Black with a silver cane. She had determined the defense—romance always touched the hearts of jurors—and her plan was that after a year's retirement, she would return to the stage, more loved then before.

"Have you reached a verdict?" The Judge's face was flushed and his breath came rapidly as he spoke in a hoarse voice.

The moment was tense.

"We have, your Honor," the jury foreman answered. "Miss East . . ." in a voice filled with emotion, "is innocent of any wrong doing."

Love triumphed and pandemonium swept the courtroom . . . .

"But my return to the stage never happened. I was old news. Then after all those years in isolation, the Big One hit California and provided me with *one more* bid."

"*My* comeback," Horace whispered.

"My last chance for immortality! And now it has all blown up in my face because of you and your overweening pride. The Greeks were right. Hubris gets 'em every time."

No one said anything, no one dared interrupt. Finally she sighed—a sigh like a wheeze inhaled—and addressing Horace, said with deep resolve, "I'm going to have to dispatch you, too."

Horace felt the panic rising. He concentrated on stifling the scream welling up inside his throat. "If you do away with me, you do away with yourself."

"Don't you think I know that, Dumb bell-Dora?" The Old Woman yelled. "But you committed the one unforgivable act."

Horace's body jerked convulsively. "I'm sorry," he muttered.

"It's not enough to be sorry!" The Old Woman shouted. "You have destroyed my legacy. One more belief exploded in the face of the people. And all for what?" She spat out the words with utter contempt. "For a little jizz-jam."

"No harm is done," Horace whispered. "Wang is dead. He can never reveal . . . and you can get rid of . . ."

Pittsburgh and Mona, who had sat on the piano bench watching the scene as though they were at a movie, now realized that by "get rid of" Horace meant them.

The violent anger The Old Woman had felt now turned to sadistic bemusement as she watched Horace's panic intensify. Choosing her words carefully, she said, "I told you when I got the idea for this taping you could be *me*, but *only* if you did it with the utmost care. I never thought you might," she took a suspenseful moment, "die *before* me."

Horace put his hand to his throat.

"I knew from surveillance before I ever took you on that you had an enlarged heart." There was a smile on her face. "But one has to take *risks* and 'je ne regrette pas', as the Frog croaked. I've been lucky in my lifetime and the system has been good to me."

Horace turned slowly toward the medicine bottle on the end-table beside the sofa. Putting one hand to his throat, he reached for and unscrewed the bottle's cap. But in this desperate effort he dropped the bottle and the nitroglycerin tablets spilled out over the parquet. "Please," he gasped to Beulah. "Hand me one of those pills."

A malevolent grin spread over Beulah's big face and he folded his massive arms.

Horace fell to his knees and reached for the nearest pill, but The Old Woman, anticipating his action, drew it just out of reach with the handle of her cane. He reached again, and again she moved the pill. Horace looked up into her eyes, which revealed no pity. Turning to Pittsburgh and Mona, he said, "Please help me."

Pittsburgh started to rise.

The Old Woman raised her cane. "Sit down!"

He did as he was told.

Horace tried to rise but his knees buckled. Then, his hand clutching his throat, there came a terrible sound from deep within. He'd suffered a stroke; one side of his face went grotesquely slack.

The Old Woman watched for a moment before sitting back in her wheelchair and staring straight ahead. After a while she said in her best Bette Davis imitation, "Beulah! Beulah! Ya all come here quick."

"What is it, Miz Regina?"

"Mr. Horace has had a stroke of paralysis."

Beulah threw up her hands in mock horror and moaned. "Oh, Lordy, Lordy, me!"

"Take him into the bedroom."

Beulah dragged Horace's body toward the door. "Should I fetch de doctor?"

"Save yourself a call. Wait just a minute and you can call the undertaker."

The Old Woman shook with laughter.

Beulah took up the laugh, which turned into a full throated howl as he dragged the paralyzed body—a body in which the panicked moving eyes were the only sign of life—into the bedroom.

The Old Woman turned to Pittsburgh and Mona. "Well, what are you staring at?" she demanded.

"It's . . . it's . . . just . . . that I have a feeling I've seen this happen before." As Pittsburgh spoke it came to him that he and Mona were now alone with The Old Woman. Taking Mona's hand he started toward the door.

"And where do you think you're going?" The Old Woman asked, smiling.

"I thought," Pittsburgh said nervously, "that Mona and I would just slip down to the dining room, maybe have a bite of cottage cheese before . . ."

The Old Woman raised her cane, from which rose a small puff of smoke as the frame of the hall door splintered and fell. Turning back slowly to The Old Woman, Pittsburgh said quietly, "Maybe we'll just skip lunch."

"Did you think I would be such a fool as to be left alone, helpless and dependent on the kindness of strangers?" The Old Woman laughed.

"I just wasn't thinking," Pittsburgh said as they sank back onto the piano bench. Unconsciously and out of habit, he began to arrange the sheet music on the piano's lyre. As he did, a plan incubated in his feverish brain. "Is this the sheet music for the video?" he asked, trying to sound casual.

"Why yes," The Old Woman said. "Horace was to practice here and I was going to give him my notes from this morning's rehearsal."

"You saw it?"

"Yes, from behind the screen in the stage box."

Pittsburgh nudged Mona. "Play," he whispered, indicating the music. He turned back to The Old Woman. "You know, I agree with what you just said."

"Just said?"

"About how important it is for you to go on." He moved closer. "I mean, even if it is in the guise of another, a standby like Horace?"

"Yes," The Old Woman mused. "But that's impossible now. A pity. I suppose you'd call what happened to Horace an example of life imitating art."

Using the soft pedal, Mona started improvising a variation of the video's song to underscore the conversation between them.

Working with the music to heighten the emotion, Pittsburgh said, "Mona and I were talking only this morning. We were saying how we'd had it with the disillusionment peddlers and the muckrakers of the fourth estate."

"The way they savaged Liz Taylor," Mona explained.

"And Hillary" Pittsburgh said, beginning a kind of stichomythic effect in which he and Mona alternated examples to illustrate the point.

"Condi! Just for a little shoe fetish. Big deal!"

"Poor Rush, even though he *did* do drugs."

"And the First Lady! I mean with *him* gone all the time, who wouldn't be a desperate housewife?"

"Sex with his sox on, Eliot Spitzer."

"George and Barbara."

"Babs?" The Old Woman interrupted.

"Yes, with the pearls."

The Old Woman's eyes rolled upward. "Is nothing sacred?"

"Mark Sanford thinking the Appalachian trail was in Argentina."

"Hole in one, Tiger Woods."

"John Edwards."

"Tom Cruise and Katie Holmes."

"So as we were saying," Pittsburgh continued, "it is vital to keep the legend of April East alive."

"Yes!" The Old Woman agreed.

"I know you have lots of money and money is not what keeps you going, although, if you stop now there won't be any more money coming in. And God knows, with the war and all, our national debt in the trillions, and the Chinese about to foreclose on the White House . . ."

"A little cash flow can't hurt," Mona added, "what with stock market fluctuations, inflation, and recession." Then, lifting her foot from the soft pedal she played full-force as Pittsburgh sang in imitation of April East:

> Soooo, pull yourself up
> Brush yourself off
> And begin again once again
> Begin once again
> Begin once again
> Till you've reached the end
> Then do it again!

The Old Woman had turned slowly in Pittsburgh's direction. Sensing the advantage, he whispered in her ear while Mona played a low pedaled variation of the song. "I can do them all. Davis." He did the cigarette bit. "Hah! Garbo: 'I vant to be alone.' West: 'Come up and see me sometime.'" And then lowering his voice, "Sorry I had to slap you around, Sweetheart, but you got hysterical when I said no more."

The Old Woman was delighted. "Bogie! Perfect."

"Hepburn: 'I never realized any mere physical experience could be so stimulating.' Garland: 'Why, oh, why can't I?' Dietrich: 'See what the boys in the back room will have . . .'"

"That Kraut!" The Old Woman sneered.

"Piaf: 'Non, je ne regrette pas.'"

"Not bad, not bad at all," The Old Woman mused.

Pittsburgh could see by her eyes that she was thinking furiously.

Then Mona sang, loud and clear. "He could do it."

"All I need is a chance!" Pittsburgh sang.

Mona sold the last line. "He could do it. Ms. East could certainly see to it!"

The Old Woman plucked at the long black hair under her chin. "Maybe she could . . ."

"With your help," Pittsburgh whispered.

"Maybe, just maybe with my help." The Old Woman paused a moment, making the slow transition from doubt to acceptance. "If I could make it seamless."

"You can!" Pittsburgh said.

"But seamless takes work."

"I'll work!" Pittsburgh said, "I'll work my fingers to the bone."

"It's not your fingers I need. It's the voice box and feet," The Old Woman said. "And have you got 'the right stuff?'"

"I've got pluck and grit and courage and determination and individual initiative. I'm self-reliant, a rugged individual, and steadfast. I don't flip-flop and I can lift myself up by my bootstraps." He did a standing jeté.

"It takes all that and more," The Old Woman said.

"What?"

"Ruthlessness!" Her voice was like gravel.

Mona improvised a ruthless variation of the music as Pittsburgh demonstrated ruthlessness.

"And for those who succeed . . ."

"What? Tell me!" Pittsburgh begged.

The Old Woman spoke very simply. "A great heart."

"Let me tell you about my heart," Pittsburgh said as Mona shifted to a lyric variation of the melody.

"When I was little, I used to go to a field in back of where we lived," he said to The Old Woman.

"Yes?"

"There was a clover patch in a field of green."

"Yes?"

"I looked up at the great fleecy, white clouds."

"Yes?"

"I daydreamed."

"That's it! That's what *I* did, daydreamed!" The Old Woman said, the ferocity in her voice gone.

"I dreamed about when I would be noticed! The dream was to be rich and famous, and later it changed to get even with all the people who'd been mean to me. And then—I can't remember exactly when—but as I grew older the dream became more specific and finally, it had to do with . . ."

⌒⌒

It's the Dorothy Chandler Pavilion in Hollywood on Award Night. Pittsburgh exits from a black stretch limo.

Mary Hart of *Entertainment Tonight* is waiting to interview him. Pia Lindstrom shoves a microphone in his face.

Fans wave.

The presentation.

The master of ceremonies lists him as one of the five nominees.

The envelope is opened. A young Barbara Stanwick announces, "The winner is . . . Pittsburgh O'Casey!"

There is thunderous applause. The orchestra, under the direction of Ray Block, plays a turgid Puccini/Andrew Lloyd Webber version of the video's theme song. Pittsburgh restrains tears. He is hugged by members of the profession as he leaves his row to ascend to the platform. Barbara Stanwick kisses him and hands him the golden Oscar. At the podium, he tries to contain his emotions.

"This is a dream come true," he says. "I've dreamed all my life of this moment and now it's here. I've sometimes been annoyed with recipients who have thanked so many people, but I'm certain tonight that you, the members of the Academy, will indulge me if I take the time to thank . . . First, I want to thank my mother and fa . . .fa . . . fa . . . ther." He stops short, gripped with emotion. The truth is he doesn't know that many people. "My friend, Mona LaMode, and well. . . everyone! The members of my union . . . I'm proud to be a part of . . . and I thank you, the members of the Academy, for voting for me . . . as the best . . . pillow plumper in Hollywood . . . ."

⌒

Mona played a loud Te Deum that brought Pittsburgh back to reality.

"Well," said The Old Woman, "my dream was to become an American Legend."

"And I can do that for you," Pittsburgh said. "At the Awards, I'll say, 'I have come back. April East has come back to give of her talents to aid the victims of our great disaster. And I thank you for giving me your highest award.'"

The Old Woman had been removing a costume from a box. "This is what I wore in the old days. Now I will show you how the number is done. Wrapping herself in the faded glory of the red, white and blue bunting, holding the torch, and placing the seven spiked Miss Liberty crown on her head, she turned to Mona. "Hit it!"

Mona played in slow time, accompanying The Old Woman as she went through a kind of dance macabre, her pendulous breasts swaying under her blouse.

When she had finished, panting and out of breath, she said, "As you can see, I stole a lot of it from Jimmy Cagney in *Yankee Doodle Dandy*. Now, you try it."

Pittsburgh went through the bit in regular tempo.

Beulah returned and stood for a moment observing the smile of satisfaction on The Old Woman's face. He knew what was happening and he knew his time had not yet come, that for awhile the power he sought—had been seeking for so long—would be delayed. "What's going on?" he asked casually.

"Aristotle was right," The Old Woman said. "Everyone loves a reversal scene! April East is alive and well and will perform this afternoon."

⌒◯

What followed was a montage of Pittsburgh's preparation.

He went over and over the steps as The Old Woman gave instructions. He was sweating, not only from the work but from what he was thinking. Wang had been murdered. The Old Woman had caused Horace to have a stroke. She was planning to murder J.O. Could murder, most foul, go unpunished?

Well, maybe it could.

"That's not it!" The Old Woman yelled. "You're not concentrating!"

"Sorry."

"Where's your mind?"

"I was thinking of the costumes."

"What about them?" The Old Woman asked.

"The ones in Horace's dressing room."

"Yes?"

"Last night, after they arrived, I helped on the unloading and later, after everyone was gone, I tried a couple of them on."

The Old Woman was pleased. "Initiative!" she said to no one in particular. "Did they fit?"

"Like a glove," Pittsburgh said. "But the one for the first number, the Civil War, isn't quite right."

"I saw it," The Old Woman said, "and agree. But as much as I hate expedience, I'm afraid it is going to have to do. That is, unless you have a suggestion."

Do I ever, he thought. He went to the Tudor windows, sat, and leaned his head against the green velvet curtains he had selected for the taping. "I think I have," he said.

"What is it?" The Old Woman asked.

"The first number needs something more authentic, more traditional."

The Old Woman agreed. "Before the transition into the others."

"Exactly. Something rich, something historic that would be recognized as the style from the Civil War period, different from any of the others, especially the Miss Liberty outfit."

"Well, what's your idea?" The Old Woman asked.

He leaned back and touched the moss-green velvet curtain. It felt both prickly and soft beneath his cheek and he rubbed his face against it like a cat.

Mona started—at first very low—playing the theme music from *Gone With The Wind*. Slowly, as the music increased in volume, Pittsburgh looked at the curtain. He had brought the dress with him. It might need a little fixing—Miss Vivian Leigh had only a twenty-six inch waist—but a tuck here, a gusset there, some added material . . .

He rose from the window seat and in pantomime of a tremendous pull, yanked the curtain from its rod and held it to his body.

Beulah caught on immediately. Looking disapprovingly and with deep suspicion, he moved in on Pittsburg and in his best Mammy voice, said, "Whut you up to wid Miss East's po'teers?" Then girding himself for mock-combat, he added, "You ain't got no bizness wid Miss East's po'teers! Juckin' de poles plumb outa de wood, an' droppin' dem on de flo' in de dus. Miss East set great sto' by dem po'teers an' ah ain't tendin' ter have you muss dem up dat way."

"Fiddle-de-dee!" Pittsburgh said, and gave Beulah a slight shove. "Scoot up to the attic and get that box under my bed in which is the only thing I could save when the disaster struck. It's Mr. Walter Plunkett's." Giving a wink, he added, "And maybe his *son* Lee's original creation." He turned to The Old Woman. "It will take too long to explain, but I just happen to have the original with me."

The Old Woman paused for a moment, then smiled. "If you do, that fact rips the long arm of coincidence right out of its socket."

She thought a moment and added, "But nothing surprises me anymore." She turned to Beulah. "After you scoot up to the attic for this costume, scoot right back here."

"What for?"

"To Get Horace, what's left of him. You and I are going down to the basement." Then turning to Pittsburgh, she said, "Let me have your ring, dear."

He removed the Carnegie Tech alumni ring from his third finger, right hand, and handed it to The Old Woman.

Chapter XII

As the great creaking oak door opened, cobwebs reflected the light, and bats fluttered until they found darkness at the backside of ceiling beams. The two made their way down the stairway, Beulah carrying Horace's paralyzed body, The Old Woman carrying a small pillow and her cane and grasping the railing for support.

The hotel's basement was a great dungeon seldom frequented. On orders from J.O. North, it had been designed as a replica of Chancellor Otto von Bismarck's Bavarian castle basement at Hohenzollernsten, the use for which, historians differed. Enormous stone steps formed a stairway leading downward to a central room through which one entered via vaulting arches. Only the light from the open door above illuminated the descending steps and the room below with its great furnace.

On her order, Beulah stripped Horace Mann's paralyzed body. When he was naked, The Old Woman indicated the furnace door with her cane.

Beulah opened it, leaned down. and was about to lift Horace when she cried, "No, Fool! The clothing. Just the clothing."

Beulah threw the clothing, piece by piece, into the furnace. Licking flames shot upward as Horace's frantically shifting eyes delighted The Old Woman. She had planned it this way. He would be thinking he was next, but cremating him alive would be too painless a death. Instructing Beulah to carry his body to the open gate of the elevator shaft, she directed that the body—legs and arms spread wide—be placed at the very center of the shaft. Handing Beulah the pillow, she told him to place it under Horace's head at such an angle so she could see his eyes but that he could still look upward. Beulah then slipped Pittsburgh's college ring on to his third finger, right hand.

Waiting a delicious moment so Horace could clearly see and know where he was, she pressed the down button that triggered the iron monster's slow creaking descent. A smile spread over her wrinkled face as from just outside the shaft, she watched the frantic darting eyes as they looked up at the rusty iron spikes drawing closer and closer. Horace tried desperately to move but was unable. Only his brain was alive and capable of functioning as the spikes draw nearer. Then there was the moment when he first felt them, their slow entrance into his flesh like a thousand needles and then the weight of the monster settling ever so slowly to a few inches above the floor, flattening its obstruction.

He had betrayed her confidence. Twice!

She waited impatiently for just the right amount of time before lifting her cane to push the up button to the seventh floor. At her command, the monster reacted with just the slightest hesitation, a quiver as delicate as the lid of a waffle iron that, having received raw batter, was being raised precipitously before the top of the waffle was fully baked. Then, the thing attached to its lid, was released by the spikes and dropped back onto the stone floor.

What dropped was the enlarged flattened-out-to-a-few-inches-thick body of Horace Mann, looking like a gingerbread cookie, or perhaps, because of the dripping blood combined with crushed bones, marrow and other bodily fluids, more like a freshly cubed steak, lying there in the perfectly formed if distended shape of a human being.

She cackled in delight. "I think that does it." She turned to Beulah. "And now," she proclaimed, "on with the show!"

Chapter XIII

Outside the Bijou, a militant group of protesters, mostly college kids, were trying to interrupt the taping. A rag-tag Cox's army with an aura of left-over- Sixties, a cross between Greenpeace and Free Choice, they carried banners reading, "Protest Lady Liberty T-Shirts!" "Materialism Runs Amuck!" and "Capitalistic Greed!"

Media provocateurs under the mantra "Fair and Balanced" were praying for a confrontation between the protesters and the true believers. Pictures of the two sides getting knocked on their asses would be a story for which their public would go crazy.

Inside the Bijou the cry of the mob could be heard over a cacophony of sounds in preparation for the off, now on-again, taping.

Rimsky Horowitz pounded the piano as the dancers, Peter, Dick, Putz and Wang's twin brother, Dong, rehearsed.

"You think you got it?" Peter asked Dong.

"I got it."

"Sorry to work you so hard but . . ."

"Is OK. Grateful for opportunity in America."

The noise was driving Nick nuts. Smiting his forehead, he yelled to Suzie, "Problemi, sempre problemi!"

Sitting on the lip of the parquet platform working on alterations for the green velvet dress, Mona asked, "What's he talkin'?"

"He says there are always problems. First the taping is on and then it's off, and now it's. . ."

"Miss East is in her dressing room, isn't she?" Mona said, continuing to stitch. "So it's on."

"But won't the noise outside interrupt the taping?" Suzie asked.

"They've rigged big screens out there so the crowd will see the show as it takes place. They'll be quiet when it starts."

"Not the protesters!"

Mona stopped stitching. "What's happening out there?"

"There's a small crowd protesting the selling of April East as Lady Liberty, which is an iconic patriotic statue and which she is wearing as a costume. They may have a point."

"What point, Luv?"

"Exploitation. The commercialization of the idea of liberty."

Mona threw down her sewing. "Commercialization? You're talkin' the long costume, the robe and the spiked . . ."—she demonstrated with her hands behind her head, seven fingers straight up—". . . headdress, standing for the seven continents and seas?"

"Yes," Suzie said. "They say it's like using the image of the smoldering ruins of Chicago's recently bombed Sears Tower as background to make a buck."

"Excuse my French, but *Bullshiiit!*" Mona said, rolling the cardboard from the orange blossom box into a cylinder and heading up the aisle.

☙

In the square in front of the theatre, waving small American flags, there were thousands, not only from Timbuckone and the Dakotas but from Chicago, New York, and Los Angeles. The foreign press and television were also represented, especially the Italian paparazzi, all of them to celebrate, support and exploit the taping.

The much smaller group of protesters, having been unable to get in the stage door, had moved to the front of the theatre and were about to storm its great oaken doors when they were flung wide and Mona emerged, moving out onto the portico where she held up her hand. The crowd grew silent. Using the cardboard megaphone, she shouted, "I hear a few of you folks are angry because some enterprising Indians are out hustling T-shirts and doodads so they can make a few bucks while Miss East's in town."

Affirmative responses rang from the protesters.

"You call that exploitation?"

"Yes!" came the roar from the few.

"Well, so it is, Luvs! What do you think this country's all about? It was founded on the idea of free enterprise. So out here in the Dakotas the free enterprisers are selling April East, Lady Liberty T-shirts for twenty-five bucks apiece. That ain't exploitation; that's commerce. What the hell does Miss Liberty stand for if it's not freedom to make a buck?"

There was an instant roar of affirmation from the vast majority crowding the square. Mona turned to the dissidents. "You hear that? It's you college kids and your egghead professors promoting their half-assed Sixties ideas that's screwing things up. And what I say is if you don't like what's happening, you know what you can do? Take it to the Supreme Court!"

Another thunder of approval.

"Why do you think foreigners want to come here? Why do you think they're jumping off ships out in the harbors and swimming ashore? Why do you think they're swarming in over the borders from Mexico? Why do you think they're taking off in inner tubes from Haiti and Cuba? Everyone's trying to get into the good ole U.S. of A!"

A great lusty cry came from the crowd.

"Half of Eastern Europe. Hell! Three quarters of South Americans want to come here. And why?"

Although she was a very small figure against the facade of the Bijou, Suzie stood tall as she listened to Mona's tirade.

"What does the Statue of Liberty stand for?" Mona yelled. "'Give me your tired, your homeless, your wretched masses.' And what does April East stand for?"

To exploit the lowest common denominator, Suzie thought.

Mona paused for only a moment before answering her own question. "What April East and Miss Liberty stand for is freedom to make a buck! That's the bottom line."

Suzie shook her head.

"And as an Australian-American, I don't see anything wrong with that. So stop your whining." Mona blasted her conclusion. "You're obstructing free enterprise!"

Another roar went up from the throats of the majority who, incited by her rant, moved in on the protesters. Suzie saw the beginning of the violence: young people hit, knocked to the ground and trampled. Before she ran back into the theatre, she saw the tall blue-eyed Clem and his two deputies move in to restore order.

"I have it. Yes, I have it!" Dong said excitedly to Peter.

"Nick!" Suzie called.

Nick ignored her. "Maestro?" he asked Rimsky.

"Tutto pronto, Signor Sabbatini," Rimsky answered.

Nick turned to one of the properties people. "Ho bisogno di fiori freschi!" he ordered.

Suzie was horrified. "Fresh flowers? You want fresh flowers now? Look at what's happening out there!"

An assistant yelled, "Pittsburgh! Pittsburgh!"

Although it was not uppermost in her mind at that moment, Suzie did wonder where Pittsburgh was. The most conscientious member of the crew, he was always there. Where was he now?

Pittsburgh was sitting in front of the makeup table in the portable dressing-room wondering what had happened to Horace Mann when he heard his name being called. Instinctively, through years of conditioned service as a set dresser, he started to rise. From the corner, The Old Woman moved her cane, directing him to be seated. "The call is from one of the assistant stage managers ordering you to do something on the set. Crushed to death in an elevator accident and identified by the ring on his finger, Pittsburgh, the pillow plumper, is dead," she said.

Sinking back onto his chair Pittsburgh looked at his reflection. He had skillfully applied the foundation, the mascara, the rouge. He was beginning to *be* April East, or would be just as soon as he finished with the eyelashes and wig. Let them get someone else to do whatever needed to be done. He had bigger fish to fry.

And as for Wang's murder, Pittsburgh did not know what to do, nor did he know exactly how he should feel about what happened to Horace. But were these really matters for his concern? *He* had done nothing wrong. He had always been essentially non-political, an artist, politics beyond him. He'd think of the politics of it tomorrow.

Skillfully lifting the fragile eyelash onto his lid, he thought of what The Old Woman had said: the eyelash, the wig, the makeup was just the outer façade; it was the inner quality that made an April East. And what was that? Well, it was many things, including ruthlessness.

⌒⌒

Sheriff Clement Jones, after quelling a near riot with his deputies, entered the stage door. Politely removing his hat, he asked an assistant if he could speak to someone in charge.

As the sheriff was waiting, the wizened man-boy, J.O, frazzled and exhausted, burst through the door and headed straight for Nick. Seated on the edge of the parquet platform, Beulah was helping Mona attach a slash of Velcro to the moss green velvet dress. "Where the hell did he come from?" Mona whispered.

"Nick!" J.O. called as he slithered toward the director.

Beulah rose. "Mr. J.O," she said, her voice falsely pleasant, "you git over here dis minute."

J.O stopped. "No!" he yelled hysterically. "You locked me in the bathroom where I almost died of suffocation!"

Beulah moved toward him. "What you talkin' 'bout, boy?"

"I'm gonna tell on you," J.O. raged. "I'm gonna tell everything, about her and Wang."

"Tell? Tell what?" Suzie asked. She turned to Nick. "What's he saying?"

Beulah advanced quickly. "Mr. J.O, what you carryin' on about?"

J.O. started running. In the stage box out of view of the audience, The Old Woman had taken her place to watch the taping. Now, she sprang from her chair and took aim. The sudden motion of the cane's metallic barrel caught and reflected the light. Beulah looked in the direction of the box as an ever-so-slight puff of blue smoke coiled upward. Looking back, she saw J.O's stunned look and silent scream. Reaching a claw-like hand up and around, he clutched his shoulder and started moving backward. Beulah moved toward him as Mona surreptitiously reached out and removed the pin from the rusty hinge of the trap door. J.O.'s frail body, with its terrified face, bulging neck veins and the open mouth that denied the scream, plummeted into the theatre's cellar. Beulah moved quickly to the splintered trap lid. "Snakes! Side-winding their way, then striking!"

"Ci sono delle vipere?" Nick asked.

"Snakes?" Suzie repeated almost to herself.

"Ohhhhhh, Lordy! Lordy!" Beulah moaned, looking down into the trap. "Poor Mistuh J.O.'s done gone. The snakes done got him!" Making a keening sound, she moved slowly off stage toward the dressing room.

"Che ci faceva una vipera lá?" Nick asked.

Looking into the cellar, Suzie cried, "Help him! Someone help him!"

Clem stepped forward, but even as Suzie called for help, she saw the frail body of J.O. give a last furious tremor as life left it. "There were no snakes. I didn't see any snakes. How can he be dead?" Except for this select group, the crew was so busy with final details that they were not aware of what had just happened.

"It's a tragedy," Mona said, "but life goes on."

Clem had taken Suzie gently by the shoulders to stop her from moving in circles. Suzie looked at Mona unbelievingly. "We'll have to tell April what has happened!"

"What good can telling her do now?" Mona asked.

"Che cosa?" Nick asked.

"Dead is dead!" Mona said. "No point in upsetting her now. We can tell her afterwards."

"But she must know," Suzie said.

"What can she *do* about it?" Mona asked.

"But it's the decent human thing."

"No, Luv!" Mona said. "I once worked for a director who told the cast that if anything terrible happened to either one of us or our relatives prior to the performance, we would not be notified until after the final curtain.

"That's inhumane."

"No, that's show business," Mona said. At that very moment, a switch was activated and the parquet floored platform started tracking downstage.

Nick checked his watch. It was zero hour. "Attenzione! Silenzio! La Signoria East è pronta!" he called to the cinematographer.

The platform continued downstage, covering the gaping hole in the stage floor. Lights were coming on, the HOLLYWOOD backdrop was flying in. The taping was about to commence. "L'orchestra è pronta?" Nick asked Shephard Thomas. On the set, Nick called, "Silenzio! Ciak, si gira!"

From all over the house and in the public square assistant stage managers repeated the call. "Quiet!" "Quiet on the set!" "We're gonna roll." "Quiet!" The calls echoed in the distance. And then there was nothing but silence.

Putting on the earphones, Nick headed to the back of the theatre. "Che lo spettacolo inizi!"

Suzie looked into the clear blue eyes of Clement Jones. "Can we talk?"

"Yes, Ma'am."

⌒⊙

April East made her way through the throng of technicians toward the set in her GWTW costume, followed by Mona. The stage was like a cobra, drawing her to it, beckoning with flicking tongue. As she moved, she felt strangely as if there were something inevitable about the moment, that all her life had been a preparation for what was about to take place. She heard the gasps of approval from the crew as she moved into the light. Once on stage, Mona took her hand and squeezed it. "Neck and leg break, Luv," she whispered and then took up her position at the right proscenium arch just out of camera range.

"Are you ready, Miss East?" someone asked.

Using Gary Gilmore's words to his executioner, she answered, "Let's do it!"

Standing beside Clem, Suzie felt paralyzed. There was no stopping what was about to happen.

Chapter XIV

The silence was electric, broken only by the hollow lifeless sounds of instructions given over headsets by the stage manager and Nick. Then, the moment of beginning. The taping commenced.

April East snapped her fingers to the rhythm and sang of the Civil War, followed by the 1906 San Francisco Earthquake, The Great Depression, World War II, the assassination of John F. Kennedy, the bombing of the World Trade Center and the killing of Osama Bin Laden.

Production values were mainly in the change of costumes for each segment, starting with Scarlett's going-to-meet-Rhett gown and finishing with the Statue of Liberty outfit. The muscle men wore red, white, and blue abbreviated shorts enhanced with cod pieces.

The visual setting was April's Hollywood studio for each of the episodes—which she occasionally used—but kept the focus on the ten syllable line lyrics which were written in a theatrical show-business manner that included rhymed couplets: "The Rebs lost the war, and the South evermore," "A sweat shop on fire, and Children perspire," "Lus'tania sank, Doughboys outflanked," "The market went bust, with plenty of dust," "Pearl Harbor alight, not a pretty sight." "Guadalcanal, and Normandy sail," "The A-bomb explodes, and Korea froze," "Kennedy boys shot, Martin Luther plot," "Saigon, Vietnam, and Cold War du jour," "Apollo in flames,

Guys without dames," "Twin Towers explode, and Senators probe," "We sock Iraq, causing plenty of flack," "Katrina got mean in New Orleans," "Osama bin Laden, was really an odd one," And finally. . . "Hollywood gone, like a dying swan."

At the end of each disaster was a repeated (with slight variations) verse of ten lines describing America's reaction to it:

> So what did we do?
> Moan and cry
> Throw up our hands
> Lay down and die?
>
> Hell no! Cause . . .
>
> No one ever said
> It would be easy
> No one ever said
> It wouldn't be hard
>
> Soooooooooooooooo

Followed by a seven line finale, always the same:

> Pull yourself up
> Brush yourself off
> And begin once again
> Begin once again
> Begin once again
> Till you've reached the end
> Then do it again!

Occasionally throughout, in a riff as in Puccini's *Madam Butterfly,* the razzmatazz stopped and April East sang in the glorious classic manner, "Oh, say can you see, by the dawn's early light, *once* so proudly we hailed at the twilight's last gleaming . . ."

After her show biz narrative of the final disaster—the end of Hollywood— she gave it her all.

> So whatta we gonna do?
> Grumble and whine?
> Beat on our breasts?
> Let America decline?
>
> Hell no, cuzzzzzz

And then a change to the half time rag ending, slowing down to start and building the song in time and force to a knock-their-sox-off blaze of glory with spectacular fireworks and images of a gigantic American flag waving over fields of grain.

The final note sounded and then silence.

"Aspetta che controlliamo," Nick yelled and came down the aisle from the back of the theatre talking into his headset. "Tutto bene? Ci sono stati dei problemi?" Although legend had it that April East was a one-shot-take, everyone in the theatre waited for the confirmation. "OK!" Nick said. Then, removing the headphones, he gave a thumbs up sign, "È finito! È . . . It's a wrap!"

There were rebel yells and back slapping and laughing among the technicians. Nick took April East's hand and led her stage-center. The odd thing was that even as it was happening, Pittsburgh felt perfectly natural being led by Nick into the limelight. The applause, the cheers, the genuine love that came from this audience of showbiz professionals was heartfelt. And approval from one's peers—especially the tech guys—was the best support one could hope for.

Bowing low before them then raising up and looking to etch the scene forever in his memory, he bowed once again. The ovation became louder and it was difficult to keep the tears from his eyes. This was the moment he had been waiting for his entire life. Turning, he motioned for the muscle men to step forward and join him. It was the graciousness of this gesture, of sharing applause, that would endear him. And when the sound of the acceptance became even greater, he held his right hand straight out, palm up, to Rimsky and then to Shephard Thomas and finally to Nick, and he and the dancers led the applause. Stepping forward again, he took a bow and this time when he raised up, he turned and left the stage. The pandemonium continued as though April East would take another curtain call.

At the proscenium arch, Suzie and Clem were the only ones not applauding. Nick had followed his star until she disappeared into the portable dressing room with Mona. He stood in the wings hoping she would return to take another call so he could escort her to the stage. But she did not return. He stood there even after the applause had ended. When he turned back to the stage, the strike— the dismantling of the set, the removal of the lighting instruments and the general restoration of the stage—was in full swing.

Although construction and set-up had taken almost two weeks, the destruction of it took very little time. And for once, the crew was not as concerned with "golden time" as they were with getting the hell out of this one-horse Dakota town.

Nick had been running on nerves for days. He could feel the wound-up tightness and heat in his groin. What he wanted was to fuck April East's brains out.

On the other side of the stage, Suzie looked as if in shock. Nick moved to her. "She looked terrific but somehow, this morning, I hadn't noticed the slight scar on her leg," he said, "not that it made any difference."

"If J.O. was bitten down there . . ." She looked toward the trapped area replaying the scene in her mind. "If he was bitten down in the trap, why did it look like he was struck from behind in his shoulder?"

Nick was not listening. He was watching the door of the portable dressing room in which his star had disappeared. "You look at her and you think she's just another good lookin' older broad who wants to get laid, but during the act, I looked through the lens—that's when I noticed the scar on her leg—and I saw something I had never seen before: her incredible vulnerability."

"When I looked down at him in the basement, I didn't see any snakes," Suzie said.

The parquet-floor covered platform was tracked up stage as the Ravenworld setting was being dismantled.

"Have you ever seen such legs?" Nick stopped suddenly. "Funny, I noticed a scar this afternoon and it wasn't there this morning when she took that spill. . ."

Suzie was watching Clem oversee the removal, by two deputies, of J.O.'s body when she said, "The legs! That was what was different! Yes! There was a scar but at this morning's rehearsal, April East was not wearing stockings and there was no scar."

Nick's gaze was still on the portable dressing room. "The legend continues!" he said. "And it will live forever!"

"I don't think so," Suzie said.

It passed through Nick's mind that there was something unaccountably new in her voice as she said it, something of resolve and ending.

Bemused, he turned. "You don't think so?"

"No, I don't think so."

"Oh, come on, Babe, lighten up!" He needed her and put his hand on her arm.

She did not say it angrily when she said, "Take your hand off me," and smiled when she noticed Clement Jones was looking at her. She moved toward him.

Nick watched her go and shrugged. Going into the auditorium, he suddenly felt exhausted and sank into an aisle seat. He sat there for a very long time watching the winding down of the strike. He watched as the stage manager brought on the ghost light that illuminated the stark reality of the back stage. As he left, the light caught the whiff of smoke from his cigarette which lingered momentarily and then . . . vanished.

In the wing he heard the old card players.

"What's the game?"

"Five card draw."

"Ante up."

"Hit me with two."

THE END

About the Author

J oe Stockdale, a Purdue University professor and artistic director for its AEA and League of Resident Theatre Company (1964-1970) is Professor and Dean emeritus, Theatre & Film, School of the Arts, SUNY, Purchase, N.Y. As such, he helped launch the careers of hundreds of students who became successful in the various worlds of entertainment.

His memoir, *Stages*, was published in 2013, and he is author of a novel, *Taking Tennessee to Hart*, a theatre history *The Man in the Spangled Pants*, and co-author of *The Architecture of Drama*. He has written a half dozen produced plays, was a contributing editor for *TheaterWeek* magazine, wrote articles for *Playbill, Equity News*, and a best-of-the-year short story for *Argosy* magazine.

He and his wife Robin, married for 67 years, live in Kalamazoo, Michigan, and are blessed with five wonderful kids, six grandsons, five great granddaughters, and one brand new great grandson.

www.ingramcontent.com/pod-product-compliance
Lightning Source LLC
Chambersburg PA
CBHW060834120626
46557CB00001B/495